PRAISE FOR IRIS MORLAND

PETAL PLUCKER

Funny, charming, and utterly captivating! I devoured this sparkling read.

— ANNIKA MARTIN, NEW YORK TIMES BESTSELLING AUTHOR

Petal Plucker was funny, entertaining, fresh and fan-yourself-worthy . . . Their enemies-to-lovers romance is both charming, tender and steamy, and you'll love both of these characters (and their families!) and their sigh-worthy happily ever after.

— MARY DUBÉ, CONTEMPORARILY EVER AFTER

Morland has created a masterpiece of a romance . . . one of my favorite [books] of the year.

— CRISTIINA READS

Humorous, raunchy, and refreshing, Petal Plucker has rightfully earned its way, in my opinion, as one of the best romantic comedy [books] this year.

— CAROL, TIL THE LAST PAGE

My One and Only

This book was gripping, well written & the chemistry between the characters sizzled throughout this wonderful read.

— AMAZON REVIEW

All I Want Is You

Another heartfelt, steamy, terrific story. This is an author who really knows how to create a story that catches a reader's attention and characters that capture her heart.

— BOOKADDICT

TAKING A CHANCE ON LOVE

Thea and Anthony are in for a surprise when it comes to the language of the heart . . . I am in awe.

— HOPELESS ROMANTIC BLOG

Then Came You

This story really pulled all my heartstrings. This was truly a beautiful story and makes you believe there really is true love out there.

— MEME CHANELL BOOK CORNER

ALSO BY IRIS MORLAND

ROMANTIC COMEDIES

HE LOVES ME, HE LOVES ME NOT

PETAL PLUCKER

WAR OF THE ROSES

~

LOVE EVERLASTING

including

THE YOUNGERS

THEN CAME YOU

TAKING A CHANCE ON LOVE

ALL I WANT IS YOU

MY ONE AND ONLY

THE THORNTONS

THE NEARNESS OF YOU

THE VERY THOUGHT OF YOU

IF I CAN'T HAVE YOU

DREAM A LITTLE DREAM OF ME

MY ONE AND ONLY

THE YOUNGERS

IRIS MORLAND

BLUE VIOLET PRESS LLC

This book was one of the hardest to complete, only because life hit me hard and fast in 2018. Thanks so much to my family and readers for giving me a reason to keep writing.

MY ONE AND ONLY

CHAPTER ONE

After ten takes that lasted throughout the morning and into the afternoon, Lucy Younger heard her stomach growl so loudly that she was pretty sure anyone within a five-mile radius would've heard it, too.

"Cut!" yelled the director, Jim Stanton. Jim had a swath of silver hair that tended to expand outward as the day progressed. Lucy wondered if it was from the humidity, or if Jim's hair expanded as he got more irritable with every take that he inevitably hated. It was rather like watching a cat fluff out its fur, arching and hissing at some threat.

"That's a wrap for now," said Jim. "Go get some lunch." He shot Lucy a sardonic glance, and she had a feeling he'd heard her stomach growling. Well, if he let them have lunch breaks before three in the afternoon, she wouldn't be so damn hungry!

Lucy had arrived on Hazel Island in the Puget Sound to film *The Last Goodbye* a week ago. It was her first movie, and although it was a smaller indie one, it was a huge opportunity for her. If she could stop doing small commercial bits or community theater… her heart did a little happy dance at the thought of becoming a bona fide movie star. Or at the very least, an indie darling.

Lucy grabbed a plate of food, the rest of the cast and crew milling nearby. They had filmed this scene outside, not far from the water, and Lucy inhaled the scent of salt and sand with satisfaction. Coupled with the clear blue summer sky and the warm day, it was impossible not to be happy. She couldn't stop smiling.

"Lucy!" Erin White, Lucy's castmate, grabbed Lucy by the elbow. "Did you hear that Hayden Masterson was cast?"

Lucy's eyes widened. After the film's original lead actor had dropped out suddenly, everyone had been on pins and needles, waiting to see who would be cast instead. Hayden Masterson was Hollywood's biggest actor, and after an Oscar nomination this year for a widely acclaimed role, he was the talk of the town.

Lucy had gotten to meet Hayden in person a year ago at a cast party another actress had invited her to. Lucy had been tongue-tied and nervous, but Hayden had gone so far as to ask Lucy about her work and to buy her a drink. He'd been so handsome that Lucy had almost swooned at his feet. When their fingers had brushed after he'd handed her a drink, she'd fallen head over heels for him.

She'd been crushing on him ever since. She even had his photo as her phone's background, and she might also have bought herself a signed photo from his website for her birthday.

"Are you serious?" said Lucy.

Erin nodded. "I just talked to the casting director. Hayden

is going to play Malcolm. He's coming up here in a few days to start filming!"

Lucy almost staggered, her heart pounding. She clutched at Erin's arm like Erin was a lifesaver in the middle of the wide ocean. "Are you serious? Hayden Masterson? Are you sure it's him?" she demanded.

"Yeah, I'm serious!" Erin grabbed Lucy by the shoulders. "Lucy Younger, you're going to be playing opposite Hayden Masterson. You get to *kiss* him. This is really happening, girlfriend!"

Lucy's piece of bread fell off her plate onto the ground, but she didn't care.

She'd get to see Hayden again. She'd get to know him, to act right alongside him. He wouldn't just be somebody she dreamed about every night. He wouldn't just be a handsome man in a photograph, his scrawling signature in the corner of the black-and-white headshot. It'd really be *him*. She couldn't believe it.

She didn't know how the producers had managed to get him to agree to star in this little indie film. Maybe they'd sacrificed a virgin to get him to sign on. Maybe he was bored with the bigger Hollywood movies and wanted something different. Maybe it was because Mercury was in retrograde, and wasn't that supposed to make things weird in the universe?

"What am I going to do?" Lucy shot Erin a terrified glance.

Erin laughed. "Don't look at him like you're going to puke, for one."

"Am I dreaming? Pinch me. Throw a bucket of ice water on me."

Erin pinched her so hard that Lucy yelped.

"Okay, okay, it's real! No more pinching," said Lucy.

Erin flashed her a grin. A pretty woman with auburn hair and an exuberant laugh, Erin had become Lucy's friend after they'd had one ridiculous conversation about their favorite cat memes. Erin had a smaller part in the film than Lucy, who'd somehow managed to get the lead role despite not having any movie experience. Lucy's resume, though, was as long as her arm, with parts in anything her agent could land her: commercials, plays, short indie flicks and everything in between.

Lucy had played everything from a woman dying of cancer to a crazy stalker ex-girlfriend to a dumb blond friend. If you printed out a list of stereotypical roles for women in Hollywood, Lucy had done them all. She'd recently done a commercial where she was a woman suffering from irritable bowel syndrome and had found the perfect medication to treat it. That had been both a highlight and a low point in Lucy's not-so-illustrious career. It had taken her close to nine years— Lucy had just turned twenty-seven earlier in June—to snag a role like this.

"Ten more minutes and we're going to start the next scene," said Jim as he passed by Lucy. "Head over to wardrobe to get changed."

Lucy wolfed down her food in record time. Checking the time, she realized that she had five minutes to change before Jim would yell at her for being late. She hurried to the costumes trailer without looking where she was going.

As she wrenched open the trailer door, she ran straight into a hard, muscular chest.

"Whoa there," said a deep male voice, large hands steadying Lucy.

Lucy looked up—and up, and up—to see laughing blue eyes gazing down at her. Although the man wasn't classically handsome, he was certainly striking with those eyes of his. With his dark hair and cleft chin, he could easily be featured in the pages of a magazine as a fashion model, lounging around in clothing that cost more than Lucy made in a year. Lucy had done a few modeling projects in between acting gigs, and this guy fit the profile exactly. He even smelled expensive.

"I'm used to women throwing themselves at me," the man drawled, his voice like velvet against Lucy's skin, "but this is a bit much." His gaze traveled from her face to her chest before taking a leisurely survey of her entire body.

Lucy blushed, irritation flashing in her eyes. Of course she'd run into some schmuck when she was in a hurry. Hopping away from him, she replied crisply, "I need to get into the trailer."

He clucked his tongue. "Not even one little sorry for practically running me over?"

Lucy rolled her eyes and tried to push past him. "I'm not a liar, so no, I'm not apologizing because I'm not sorry."

The man leaned against the door frame, effectively blocking Lucy's way. Considering he was over a head taller than Lucy's five-foot-two-inch frame, there was no way she would get around him. She growled under her breath. Why did she always have to deal with the jackasses on set?

Lucy took in the man's appearance, noting that he wore ripped-up jeans and an old t-shirt. Despite his looks, he wasn't dressed like anyone important. He looked like he could be some guy who worked behind the scenes. Besides, if he were someone important, she would've met him already. Lucy had been introduced to the producers and director the first day she'd arrived on Hazel Island.

This strange man, whoever he was, kept smiling down at her. The smile was slow and heated, and something curled in Lucy's belly. She ignored it. She didn't have time for handsome assholes making her life difficult.

"You're a little spitfire, aren't you?" he said. "I like a woman with spirit."

"Cool. I didn't ask for your opinion. And you're in my way, in case you didn't hear me the first time."

"So you've said."

Lucy crossed her arms. "What's your deal? Do you enjoy harassing random women?"

"Whoever said anything about harassing?" His smile widened, his teeth flashing.

"If this is how you pick up women, you're terrible at it."

"I caught *your* attention."

Lucy growled under her breath, and the man laughed. Finally stepping aside, he raised his arm with a flourish. "After you, little spitfire." Leaning down before she could pass by him, he whispered in her ear, "But when you see me again, try not to throw yourself at me. Men like some mystery."

Lucy glared daggers at the man's back as he laughed again and walked back onto set. But soon her costume change provided her with a much-needed distraction, the obnoxious stranger forgotten.

The afternoon's filming began with a scene with Lucy and Erin on set. Lucy's character, Miranda, was described as "an overworked career woman whose fiancé left her at the altar three months prior." In this scene, Miranda told Erin's character, Layla, how she'd run into her ex-fiancé at the local farmer's market. It had not gone well.

"He looked good," said Lucy/Miranda in a voice that became progressively higher-pitched. "Why did he look good? He should've gotten fat and sad. But he looked tan! Why is life so unfair?"

"Cut! Cut, cut, cut." Jim rose from his chair. "You sound like you're screeching," he said to Lucy. "This scene should be emotional and funny, but not ridiculous. You're playing Miranda like she's a joke. Do you think she's a joke?"

Lucy blinked. "No, of course not."

"Then stop playing her like one."

Out of the corner of Lucy's eye, she saw someone approach the set. To her immense dismay, it was the obnoxious man from the trailer. Was he stalking her now?

"Are you listening to me?" Jim's voice brought Lucy back to the present. "We don't have time to do a million takes because you don't feel like trying, Miss Younger."

"I'm sorry. I'll do better," stammered Lucy. She could feel the obnoxious man's gaze on her, and she blushed, knowing that he was seeing her get scolded like a five-year-old.

When Jim returned to his director's chair, Erin whispered to Lucy, "You got this. Jim's got a stick up his ass."

As Lucy and Erin did three more takes, Lucy watched as the obnoxious man prowled the set. With his dark hair and rangy build, he reminded Lucy of some predator, like a panther stalking its prey.

She shivered at the thought that he might be stalking *her*. But why would he? He didn't know her. He was just some guy who liked to mess around with people. She'd be better off ignoring him entirely.

After the second take, the obnoxious man brought one of the writers a cup of coffee. He must be her assistant. She had no idea why Pamela would have such an annoying assistant, or why he got to dress like a bum at work. Then again, maybe he was more useful as eye candy than actually assisting anyone.

"Do you know who that is?" said Lucy to Erin in between takes.

Erin glanced over at where Lucy had gestured. "Who? That guy?"

"Yeah. I ran into him earlier."

Erin's eyes widened, but right as she was about to speak, Jim barked, "We're doing one last take before we end for the day. Places!"

Lucy almost forgot about the obnoxious man watching her as she worked. Every time she did a scene—no matter how many takes it took—she was reminded of why she'd wanted to be an actress in the first place. Throwing herself into a character, letting herself become someone else, was one of the headiest and most addictive experiences she'd ever known.

For a while, she was no longer Lucy Younger, a nobody actress with too many bills that she needed to pay. Instead, she got to be Miranda Leighton: career woman, CEO, and a woman on a mission to move on from an ex-fiancé who'd broken her heart.

After Lucy's last line, Jim said, "That's a wrap for today. Finally, you did a take that didn't make me want to light myself on fire."

Lucy barely stifled an incredulous laugh. "Um, thanks?"

But Jim had already turned to talk to someone else. Lucy was thankful to avoid both his backhanded compliments and his wrath.

"Great job on that last take," said Pamela with a beaming smile. "That's one of my favorite scenes. I had to fight the other writers to get it included, but I finally prevailed."

Lucy smiled. "Thank you. I didn't want Miranda to come off too desperate. I was afraid my performance might be stilted."

"Not at all. You have a wonderful way of expressing yourself with just your face. I could tell exactly what you were thinking without you saying a word."

"You are very expressive," said a voice that made Lucy stiffen.

"Have you met Lucy already?" said Pamela to the obnoxious man.

He smiled that smile that made Lucy want to stomp on his foot. "Oh yes, we've met."

The way he looked at her stoked her wrath. Was he making fun of her? Lucy had put up with too many smarmy actors who'd assumed she was nothing but an easy lay to put up with this guy, too. And he was Pamela's *assistant*: he didn't get to talk to the lead actress like this. She didn't understand why Pamela wasn't telling him to back off, but maybe they had some strange relationship. Maybe they were dating.

"We ran into each other," said Lucy in a tight voice.

"Literally. Ms. Younger here practically threw herself at me." He winked.

Pamela blinked in surprise, but she didn't tell her assistant to back off. That made Lucy angrier.

"Is this how you talk to actors on set? Because if so, your approach needs some work," Lucy shot back, no longer caring about being polite.

"Lucy—" whispered Erin behind her, but Lucy ignored her.

"Yet you seem to be the one whose feathers are all ruffled," countered the obnoxious man.

Lucy curled her fingers into a fist, and she found great satisfaction in imagining punching the guy in the jaw.

"Why don't you be useful and get me a cup of coffee? That is your job, isn't it?" said Lucy scathingly, raising her voice so people could see that she was the one in control, not this asshole.

Pamela's eyebrows shot up to her hairline; Erin made a choking sound. Lucy glared up at the obnoxious man, daring him to tell her no. Assistants should *assist* people, not antagonize them.

Lucy soon realized that everyone on set had stopped what they were doing. She could practically feel their collective gazes. A blush climbed up her throat.

"Do you want cream and sugar?" said the man, his voice sweet.

Lucy squared her shoulders. "Yes. Both."

As the man went to get Lucy her coffee, Erin grabbed her arm and squeezed her so hard that Lucy gasped.

"What is it?" said Lucy.

Erin shook her. "Don't you know who that is?"

"He's Pamela's asshole assistant. Can you believe he talked to me like that?"

"Assistant? Lucy!" Erin dug her fingers into Lucy's arm so hard that Lucy yelped.

"Ow, you're hurting me—"

"You idiot! He's that huge baseball player! Didn't you recognize him? He plays for the Seattle Orcas."

Something niggled in the back of Lucy's mind. Her throat closed as dread filled her, and her palms became cold with sweat.

"Then why——?" whispered Lucy.

Right then, the obnoxious man returned and handed Lucy her cup of coffee with a sardonic bow.

"Lucy, have you met Mr. Roberts?" said Pamela in a strained voice.

Carter put out his hand, but Lucy was too frozen to shake it.

"Carter Roberts," he said in that annoying drawl, his eyes sparkling with what looked like triumph. "Baseball player turned executive producer, at your service."

CHAPTER TWO

W hen Carter's best friend, Anthony Bertram, had suggested that he work on a movie of all things, Carter had thought he was insane.

"I'm a baseball player," he'd said. "The last thing I wrote was probably some essay in the fifth grade. Also about baseball."

Anthony had waved his hand dismissively. "You won't have to write a damn thing. You'll be playing supervisor, making sure things stay on schedule and on budget. Best of all, it'll give you something to do now that you're benched for the season. I was going to do it, but I'm too busy here in Seattle with Thea and the business."

Carter had told Anthony to go find someone actually qualified. But Anthony had somehow gotten it into his brain that Carter should do the job, and when he'd told Carter he needed someone he could trust at the helm, Carter had given in. Even though Carter's interest in the movie business was about as high as his interest in the mating habits of sea anemones.

When he'd arrived on Hazel Island yesterday morning to begin the job, he'd expected to be bored out of his mind and wishing to get back to playing ball within a week.

But now, Carter was having too much fun pissing off this gorgeous little blond spitfire. Seeing her sputter in shock after she'd found out his identity was the most hilarious thing he'd experienced in a long time.

Lucy—that was her name. It fit her, Carter thought. With her pointy chin and blazing green eyes, she looked like some elfin creature he'd find deep in the woods. At the moment, her color was high, and she seemed close to punching somebody. That only made Carter smile wider.

"Are you—no, are you sure?" stammered Lucy as she shot a glance at Pamela. "Is this a joke?"

"He's the *executive producer*," hissed Pamela before she said to Carter, "I'm so sorry, Mr. Roberts. Lucy has had a long day. I'm sure she's horribly sorry for how rude she's been."

Lucy didn't look the least bit sorry this time, either, and Carter had to bite the inside of his cheek to keep from laughing. He wasn't normally the type of guy to needle a pretty girl like this, but something about the way she'd put her hands on her hips and told him to eat shit earlier had intrigued him.

Lucy visibly swallowed as she kept looking from Pamela to Carter. "I'm so sorry," she croaked. "I didn't realize."

"Oh, it's not a problem. I'm sure you can make it up to me somehow."

She squared her shoulders, muttered an apology, and promptly stalked off.

Carter wasn't mad that she was walking away: it gave him a great view of her ass, nice and round in her tight jeans.

"Mr. Roberts, I'm *so* sorry," said Pamela. Her hands fluttered in front of her like wild birds. "I'll talk to Lucy. I don't know how she didn't recognize you, but she would never have talked to you like that otherwise. But that's no excuse. I'm so sorry—"

Carter held up a hand. "It's fine. Like you said, she didn't recognize me."

Before Pamela could launch into another apologetic speech, Carter left to follow Lucy. He didn't know why he felt the need to continue to needle her.

Maybe because he'd been bored ever since he'd gotten benched after his shoulder injury. Without baseball, Carter had been set adrift, his life coming to a standstill. Not even women, parties, booze, or money could take the place of baseball in his life, no matter how much he'd partaken of all of those things.

When his good friend Anthony Bertram had asked Carter to be an executive producer for a movie he was funding, Carter had thought Anthony was losing his mind. Anthony had once been the billionaire CEO of Bertram, Sons and Co. and was now the millionaire founder of Goldfinch Press with his girlfriend Thea, so he knew a thing or two about running business ventures. That fact had only confused Carter further —why him?

What did Carter know about movies besides the fact that he liked watching them, preferably the ones that were rated R for "scenes of a sexual nature"? Nothing. He knew nothing. Anthony, though, had persuaded him to come to tiny Hazel Island for the summer to, in his words, "get off his ass and do something useful."

Carter still didn't know why he'd agreed to do the stupid thing. Maybe because Anthony had kept looking at him with pity in his eyes. *I know you're unhappy about getting benched*, his oldest friend had said, *but that doesn't mean you can sit around moping forever.*

Carter had responded that he hadn't been moping. He'd simply been at a loss how to proceed. Carter had been playing ball since he was a child, and now, at the age of twenty-nine, the thought of not playing was simply unthinkable.

It didn't take long for Carter to catch up with Lucy. She stopped in front of the steps to her trailer and turned. "Why are you following me?" she demanded. She was still flushed, her feathers still very ruffled. Carter wanted to ruffle those feathers with his own hands.

"I'm not sure your apology was sincere," he said. At her look of dismay, he barely suppressed a laugh. "I'm not the one who mouthed off at an *executive producer*, you know."

Lucy swallowed. "Please accept my apology, Mr. Roberts," she said meekly. She wrung her hands in distress.

Oh, she was good. A consummate little actress, this spitfire girl. She knew her stuff.

"You're good, you know. I've dated plenty of actresses, but you're one of the best I've seen give an apology."

Lucy's meek expression turned to anger in half a second, effectively proving Carter's theory correct. He grinned.

"You know, I've never been on a movie set," said Carter, "but from what I understand, it's not usually the executive producers who get coffee for the actors. Unless you're some big Oscar winner. Are you an Oscar winner, Ms. Younger?"

Lucy whirled on him. "In case you were wondering, I'm not sorry for what I did. You're the most pompous, arrogant—"

"That's redundant."

"—*irritating* jackass I've ever had the *displeasure* of meeting, and despite what you say, I'm not afraid of you."

That made Carter raise an eyebrow. "Why should you be afraid of me?"

"Men like you are all the same. You think women exist for your own amusement."

"You don't know anything about me, little spitfire."

She bristled at the nickname. "I don't have time for this."

"And yet, here you are."

Lucy raised her pointed chin, her lip quivering slightly. Carter suddenly wondered what that mouth would feel like against his own.

"Are you going to fire me?" she asked.

"However tempting that would be," drawled Carter, "I'm too lazy to go find a new actress and make Jim reshoot everything we've already done."

"You're a baseball player. What are you even doing here?"

Carter didn't know, but he wasn't about to tell Lucy that.

I'm bored. I'm lost. I'm nobody without baseball.

Yeah, he wasn't going to tell her any of those things.

He shrugged. "Call it expanding my repertoire."

Her green eyes narrowed as she looked at him, and Carter barely restrained himself from squirming underneath that assessing gaze. It was shrewd, distrustful, yet underneath it lurked curiosity.

Lucy's eyes widened with realization. "You're *that* baseball player."

"So you have heard of me." Triumph filled him.

He should've expected her claws, considering how he'd been playing with her. He *should* have, but when her claws sank below the surface, it still hurt.

"Last I heard, you were benched. So, is producing movies what all washed-up baseball players do in their spare time?"

Carter knew he deserved that. He knew, and yet he found himself smarting from the hurt anyway.

"You don't know a damn thing about me."

Lucy sniffed. "You're right—I don't. And I have no intention of finding out anything else about you." She peered more closely at him. "What's your game? You don't even know me. I don't know you. Don't you have fancy executive producer things to do?"

He shrugged. "Not at the moment. I was going to head back to the bed-and-breakfast, maybe go for a run. This is more entertaining."

"I'm not here to entertain you."

"But here you are, entertaining me."

Lucy lifted her chin. "I don't have time for whatever game you're playing. I have things to do. Lines to learn. You know, what I was hired to do."

Carter didn't know why he didn't let her flounce away in a huff. Was it boredom, or something else? Attraction, boredom—a distraction. Not thinking about how his career was still up in the air, and if his orthopedic surgeon didn't clear him to play, he'd have to give up professional baseball for good.

"I'm not playing anything," said Carter innocently. "You're the one getting defensive over a simple conversation."

He could practically see the steam coming from her ears. "Who in the world hired you?" she said.

"Anthony Bertram." At Lucy's widening eyes, he added, "You know the name?"

"I mean, of course I do. He's funding this project."

Lucy wouldn't look him in the eye as she said that, which

made Carter suspicious. Not that Anthony would ever cheat on Thea: Carter had seen the two lovebirds together, and they were nauseatingly happy. But he couldn't help but wonder why Lucy seemed cagey suddenly.

"Cat got your tongue now?" said Carter.

Lucy rolled her eyes. "I don't have time for this. I'm going to go work. You know, that thing people do to earn money?"

"Never heard of such a thing," he drawled.

Lucy's blond ponytail bounced as she walked away from him into her trailer, shutting the door with a slam that made Carter grin, despite wanting to yank on that ponytail a moment prior.

He didn't know how this woman managed to bring out the elementary school boy inside him. He wanted to pull on her hair and make her run after him, screaming that she'd get her revenge.

What Carter had once thought would be a boring waste of summer was suddenly becoming more interesting by the minute.

"Carter!" said Jim as Carter was about to enter his own trailer. "I want to talk to you."

Carter couldn't stand Jim Stanton, and he knew that feeling was entirely mutual. Jim had a chip on his shoulder the size of Texas that Carter had gotten this job solely through nepotism, something that Jim had told Carter point-blank during their second conversation.

"I've been wanting to talk to you since yesterday. We finally cast our lead actor," said Jim, his beady eyes glowing under his glasses.

Carter waited for Jim's point with impatience.

"We managed to get Hayden Masterson." Normally recalcitrant and irritable, Jim looked like he wanted to burst into song right then. "I can't believe it either. It took a lot of finagling, but he's going to be here within the next week."

"That's great," said Carter with little enthusiasm. "Congrats."

"I want you to be the one to welcome him." Jim said the words like he wished he could take them back. "Since you're both Hollywood people, you know."

"I'm a ballplayer, not an actor."

"You're both famous. Same difference. Hayden needs to feel like this is a real movie set, not some indie bullshit. You got me?"

Carter didn't, but he wasn't about to admit that. Smiling grimly, he replied, "You got it, Jimbo."

Hayden Masterson—of course it would be him. Carter didn't know the actor well, but a few years back, Hayden had gotten to know Carter's girlfriend at the time *very* well. Carter had been dating Rosie for three months—practically a decade for Carter—before she'd run off with Hayden, texting Carter with a brief *sorry but not sorry* message that had included three sad emojis to add insult to injury.

Carter hadn't been in love with Rosie. Considering it had been three years ago, he hardly remembered what she'd looked like. But it was the principle of the thing: having something that was yours stolen out from under your nose was unsupportable. To make things worse, the tabloids had caught onto the scandal, and it had exploded across social media. It was only when some other famous actress had gotten caught doing heroin that the public had finally looked away from Carter's humiliation and Rosie's perfidy.

Carter gritted his teeth. Oh, he'd show Hayden Masterson

a *great* time. And knowing Jim, he knew about his and Hayden's history and had asked him to be Hayden's tour guide just to be petty.

Carter wasn't new to people trying to tear him down or watch him sweat. He'd been drafted into the major leagues at the age of twenty-one and had held his own. He'd had to deal with jealous fellow players who'd wanted a kid like him to fail.

Hayden was merely a bug Carter would squash—and he'd enjoy doing it, too.

CHAPTER THREE

Lucy inhaled the scent of cinnamon rolls and coffee as she came downstairs at the local bed-and-breakfast. Most of the cast had been provided rooms here, and although it was hardly fancy, it was nice and homey and had helped Lucy relax after her stressful day yesterday.

She couldn't help but blush in embarrassment—and anger—as she thought of Carter Roberts. His stupid, grinning, handsome face, and how he seemed to love needling her as much as humanly possible. She had no idea what his deal was, and she was determined to avoid him as much as she could.

"Good morning," said Gwendolyn Parker, the owner of the Hazel Island Bed and Breakfast. Tall and curvaceous, with curly red hair, Gwen was as sweet as apple pie and probably the nicest person Lucy had ever met. It probably helped that she got to live on this beautiful island and not deal with men like Carter Roberts.

"Good morning. Those smell amazing," said Lucy. The first floor of the bed-and-breakfast consisted of the dining room, where they provided a complimentary breakfast that included local pastries made fresh every morning, and another room used for small meetings and get-togethers. The walls were a pale peach with hand-painted leaves edging the ceiling. Local artwork hung on the walls, depicting scenes of Hazel Island and more avant-garde paintings filled with slashes of color that seemed to depict nothing and everything all at once.

A few of the cast and crew were already downstairs eating along with some locals Lucy didn't recognize. Erin wasn't there yet; most likely she was still asleep, and since it was their day off, she probably wouldn't leave her room for a few more hours.

Lucy breathed a sigh of relief when she didn't see Carter. She didn't know if he was staying here, anyway. A fancy baseball player like him probably had his own place somewhere on the island.

She also couldn't believe Carter was Anthony Bertram's *best friend*. Anthony, who also happened to be Lucy's sister Thea's boyfriend. It explained why Carter had gotten this gig in the first place, but Lucy also knew that if she didn't watch herself, word would get to Thea. And then Thea would be up in Lucy's business asking all kinds of questions like the nosy older sister she was.

"Did you sleep well?" said Gwen with a bright smile. "I hope your room wasn't too cold. The windows in your room are old and tend to be drafty."

"No, it was perfect. Although I have to admit, I'd forgotten how cold the nights get here. I was spoiled in LA. Anything below sixty degrees was practically a national emergency down there."

Gwen laughed. "One of my good friends from college

moved down there, and anytime she comes up here, she wears so many layers you'd think she was in Siberia."

Lucy chose a pastry and poured herself a cup of coffee. She overheard one of the women nearby mention the name Hayden Masterson, and Lucy shivered in excitement. Hayden was supposed to arrive today. Would he be staying here? No, he'd get his own place. He was too big now to get a room at some bed-and-breakfast.

Lucy still couldn't believe the man she'd been crushing on for a year would be her castmate. Just when she'd gotten to the point where she'd seriously considered giving up acting and letting this dream go, she'd gotten the call that she'd been cast for this movie. And now Hayden was part of it. It was like the universe was telling her not to give up.

Lucy had wanted to be an actress since she'd been a little girl and had starred in her first school play. She'd been a strawberry in a play about making sure you ate your fruits and vegetables. It wasn't the most exciting role, but Lucy had loved it so much that she'd worn her strawberry costume around the house for a good month before her mom had finally put her foot down.

That had been before her mom had gotten sick. Before her father had gotten mean. Before the family had fallen apart. Lucy had been eight when Beatrice Younger had died, so her memories were less vivid than her older siblings'. Trent, Thea, Ash and Phin could remember when their mother had been happy; Lucy couldn't. Her loss had been more like a dark hole, a place that could never be filled again.

Lucy shoved away the memories. It was too pretty of a morning to wallow in the past. She was here, filming a movie with Hayden Masterson. Things were only looking up for her.

"So, Hayden Masterson," said Gwen slyly as she and Lucy sat down at a table together. "I heard the news. That's going to cause a frenzy here, you know. We're not exactly used to things like movies being filmed here."

"But it's good for business, right?" said Lucy with a bright smile. "Are you completely booked up?"

"Oh, it's been great for business. I'm not complaining, although our usuals that come up for the summer aren't too happy to be told we're booked up." Gwen's smile was wry. "I guess it's a necessary evil, all this business, you know."

"I feel very sorry for you."

Gwen wrinkled her nose and took a bite of her muffin. In the two weeks since Lucy had arrived on Hazel Island, she'd become friends with Gwen. It wasn't hard, considering that Gwen had a natural way of making people feel comfortable. It went with the territory of running a bed-and-breakfast and dealing with the public on a daily business.

"Is Hayden staying here?" said Lucy, trying not to sound too eager.

"If he were, I couldn't tell you."

"Aw, come on. I won't tell. People will find out anyway." Lucy wasn't above begging at this point.

Gwen's lips twitched. "Sorry to disappoint, but he's not staying here. We aren't exactly five-star, so I'm not offended. Plus he probably has bodyguards or whatever else famous people need. And what if there are paparazzi?" Gwen shuddered. "No thanks."

"I doubt there will be paps all the way up here."

"But there will definitely be fans with phones posting stuff online." Gwen leaned forward. "So, tell me. Do you get to kiss him?"

Lucy blushed. "Kiss who?"

"Now you're being coy. You know who I mean."

"Maybe I do."

Gwen let out a squeal that made everyone in the room turn toward their table. Lucy covered her face.

"I'm so jealous. I think I've seen every movie he's ever been in. *Going Home* is my favorite. When he comes walking through the fog and tells Janie that he loves her, I cry every single time," said Gwen.

Lucy refused to admit that she'd watched that particular scene so many times she'd lost count. Not because it was romantic, but because Lucy had marveled at Hayden's acting throughout the movie. *Going Home* had taken his career to the next level and had gotten him that Oscar nomination.

"I love that scene, but I also loved the ones where he takes his pants off," quipped Lucy.

Gwen choked on her coffee and then laughed. "You're bad, which is why I like you. Just don't think about his butt when you're doing scenes with him."

Lucy groaned, knowing that was *exactly* what she was going to think about now.

When Lucy went to get another cup of coffee and considered what she'd like to do on her day off, she froze when she saw him. No, not Hayden: Carter Roberts. Of all people…

Carter entered the dining room like he owned the place. When he spotted Lucy, he grinned lazily.

"Good morning," he said as he poured himself a cup of coffee. "Sleep well last night?"

Lucy refused to get snippy with him. That was exactly what he wanted: a reaction. "I did, thank you." She returned to her table, hoping that would put an end to the conversation.

But Carter apparently didn't get the memo as he stood over the table.

"Did you sleep well?" said Gwen to Carter.

"I did, yes. You have a great place here. When did you open it?"

"Five years ago." Gwen shot a look at Lucy, then said, "Would you like to sit down? I can pull up a chair for you."

Carter glanced at Lucy, then drawled, "No, that's fine. I just wanted some coffee to go. Have a nice day, ladies."

When Lucy finally looked over at Gwen, Gwen raised her eyebrows. "What in the world was that about?"

"Nothing."

"Really? So why do you look like you wanted to claw out his eyeballs?"

Lucy sipped her coffee. "I have no interest in Carter Roberts's eyeballs."

"Uh-huh. Well, he seemed like he'd love to enjoy more than your eyeballs, if you catch my meaning."

At that statement, Lucy choked on her own coffee. "Are you serious? He just wants to mess with me. I don't know why. I guess he's bored or something."

"So, there is a story to this. Spill, woman."

Lucy sighed and told Gwen about what had happened yesterday: Lucy not recognizing Carter and thinking he was an assistant; how she'd embarrassed herself in front of the cast and crew; how Carter had seemed intent on driving her crazy.

"He's the most arrogant, irritating jerk I've ever met, and if I didn't like you, I'd go find another place to stay so I didn't have to be near him," finished Lucy in a huff.

"Wow, and all that from yesterday. I'm impressed."

"There's nothing impressive about him or this situation. And if you're just going to be annoying—"

Gwen put up her hands, laughing. "Don't flounce off in a huff. I'm teasing you. Although I don't know why you'd be mad at somebody like *Carter Roberts* flirting with you. Did you look at him?"

"Handsomeness doesn't erase his terrible personality."

"Honey, he has more money than God, he's hot, and he's got muscles for days. Who cares about his personality?"

"I had no idea you were so shallow." Lucy smiled, though, and after telling Gwen for the thousandth time that Carter had not and would never flirt with her, she left to wander around downtown.

It was a perfect June day: cloudless blue sky, a light breeze blowing off the water not even a half mile away. Hazel Island was small enough that it consisted of one single town, and its downtown area encompassed five blocks total. The shops were like something from fifty years ago: ice cream shops, bookstores, and independent grocery stores. A clockmaker on one corner and a handmade jewelry boutique on another.

Tourists and locals alike mingled and strolled. The area was particularly busy lately due to the influx of cast and crew working on *The Last Goodbye*.

Lucy wandered into the local bookstore to peruse the shelves. The interior smelled like ink and paper, and a fat gray cat lounged in a bed near the old-fashioned cash register. When Lucy scratched behind the cat's ears, its tail swished but it kept its eyes closed.

A few other people were inside, but it was so quiet that Lucy felt like she was entering some kind of sacred shrine. Or a library on steroids.

When she reached the romance section, she had to restrain a squeal of delight when she found an array of old-school romances from the seventies and eighties in their bodice-ripping glory: in rainbow hues, the covers depicted men with bulging arms, their shirts open to the wind as women swooned in their arms. Some of the women stood in the strangest poses; Lucy had to cover her mouth to keep from giggling like an idiot.

She looked up and saw a romance from one of her favorite authors that was out of print. She stood on her tiptoes to reach it, but she was too short. She growled under her breath. This was one of many instances where she hated being short. Where was a tall person when she needed one?

She stood on her tiptoes one last time to try to reach the book—as if by sheer force of will, she'd grow three more inches in the process—when a voice said, "Let me get that for you."

A man's arm reached over her head and plucked the book from the shelf. Turning, Lucy was about to thank the Good Samaritan when she came face-to-face with Hayden Masterson himself.

Hayden. Masterson. Standing in front of her with a book titled *Seducing His Wicked Virgin*.

He looked as good as he had a year ago when Lucy had met him briefly: his hair fell over his forehead at the perfect angle to amplify his eyes, and his jaw seemed like it was cut from marble. When he smiled, it was like getting hit in the chest with a missile.

"You know, I don't know much about book titles," he said in that voice that had seduced so many women across the world, "but isn't 'wicked virgin' kind of a contradiction here?"

"Um," was the only reply Lucy could come up with.

"Although since I don't read romances, maybe you could explain. Is the virgin supposed to be wicked?" He gave her a wink that she was pretty sure made her burst into flames.

She was wondering why no one was running for the fire extinguisher when she realized she hadn't even responded to his question. "Um, usually the heroine becomes wicked once she meets the hero. It's like an awakening." Her face flamed. God, she sounded like an idiot.

"Now I'm intrigued," he said. He leaned against one of the bookshelves, all handsome nonchalance. "Maybe I should read one."

"More men should read them."

He chuckled. "What's your name? You seem familiar, but I never forget a pretty face." When his gaze slowly traveled up the length of her body, Lucy wasn't entirely certain how she was still standing. She also didn't want to point out to him that he *had* already met her. It would only make things more awkward.

"My name is Lucy Younger," she stuttered. "I'm actually your costar in *The Last Goodbye*."

His eyes widened. "What? That's where I know you from! Christ, I'm sorry. I'm an ass. You should've told me right away."

"It's fine. I wouldn't expect you to know who I was," she said honestly.

"No excuses. I need to make it up to you. How about we get a drink sometime? I think there might be two bars here. We could figure out which one is better."

"Okay," she said, sounding so breathless that she'd feel ridiculous about it if she were more coherent.

By the time Hayden said goodbye, Lucy was pretty sure she had died and gone to heaven. Hayden Masterson had asked her out. On a date! Well, not a *date* date. Just a drink between castmates. She shouldn't get too excited about that.

But excitement raced through her veins until she did a little happy dance right there in the stacks. She didn't care if she looked like an idiot. Hayden Masterson had asked her out for a drink! The man she'd been dreaming about for an entire year! She couldn't believe it. It was too good to be true.

After she'd paid for her new favorite book, *Seducing His Wicked Virgin*, Lucy stood outside the bookstore and smiled so widely that her cheeks hurt. She headed back to the bed-and-breakfast to tell Erin and Gwen about how she'd seen Hayden Masterson when she noticed a crowd had formed about a block away, near the grocery store.

Lucy hurried toward the crowd, thinking it was Hayden, but she stopped in her tracks when she realized the crowd wasn't there for Hayden: it was Carter Roberts.

CHAPTER FOUR

C arter was no stranger to people coming up to him and asking for autographs and photos. When he'd first started playing for the Seattle Orcas, he'd always been surprised whenever someone had actually recognized him. But in the years since he'd first been drafted, he'd gotten used to the attention. It came with the territory of being one of the best ballplayers in the league.

"Can I take a selfie with you?" a boy who looked maybe ten years old asked. He already had his phone out.

"Sure," said Carter. He draped his arm over the boy's shoulder, took his phone, and snapped the photo for him. That resulted in the crowd growing larger, with more and more people asking for photos.

"When are you going to play again?" a man about Carter's age asked him. "The team's playing is shit without you pitching."

Carter's good mood vanished at the reminder of his injured shoulder. "That's all the autographs and stuff for today. Thanks, guys." He waved and stepped around the perimeter of the crowd. Luckily Hazel Island simply didn't have enough people here to mob him, and they were too polite to follow him—except for the same guy who had asked him about his return.

"Do you think you won't ever play again?" the man asked, clearly on a mission to get an answer. "I've heard rumors that you tore your rotator cuff so bad that you won't ever throw again. Is that true?"

Carter, refusing to be baited despite his great desire to punch this guy in the face, said, "I know as much as you do."

"So is that a yes? Or a no?"

Carter stopped, the man almost bumping into him. "How about I tell you that it's none of your damn business? Does that clarify things for you?"

The man blinked. He finally nodded; he didn't follow Carter when he stalked away. Anger bubbled inside him: anger about his injury, about how he really didn't know if he'd ever get to play again.

Baseball was his life; it was in his blood. It had gotten him to where he was today. Without it, he would've been just some poor kid struggling to survive in a broken family. He'd probably be some alcoholic bum like his father—the father that had also seen the talent in his son and had pushed him to play baseball in the first place.

Carter had walked a block when he saw Lucy Younger. Based on her expression, she'd seen and heard everything that had just happened.

Putting on his easy grin, Carter approached her. "Following me, spitfire?" he quipped.

She shot him a confused look. "If I am, I'm obviously not very good at it."

She looked up at him through those absurdly long eyelashes she had, and it almost made Carter forget his anger. He didn't know what it was about this woman, but she was like some fairy creature he wanted to bottle for himself.

"Admit it, you're obsessed with me," he said.

"Good Lord, you're amazingly arrogant." She shot him a strange look. "What was that all about?"

"You'll have to be more specific."

"That guy following you. You looked like you were about to deck him."

"So what if I was?"

"Do you always answer a question with a question?"

That made him genuinely smile. "Only with you."

Lucy ran her finger along the spine of a book she was carrying, catching Carter's attention. He snagged the book from her grasp before she could protest. He laughed as he read the title.

"Is this what you're into? I'm surprised," he said. "Isn't 'wicked virgin' an oxymoron?"

Lucy tried to grab the book, but Carter dangled it over her head. She growled like an angry cat. "Give me my book back."

"Only if you ask me nicely."

Her green eyes sparkled, which only further improved Carter's mood. He hadn't had this much fun with a woman since…well, he couldn't remember. He'd always preferred that his women be beautiful and not much else. And there were always plenty of beautiful women around when you were an athlete. Carter had gotten to the point that he hadn't cared if a woman wanted to share in his fame or had been attracted to him because he had more money than God.

They'd always had arrangements that had suited Carter's nomadic lifestyle.

"I'm not asking you nicely. Give me my book back," said Lucy. She put her hands on her hips.

Carter considered. Feeling generous, he finally returned her book to her. "You're welcome," he said.

"Yes, thank you so much for returning the item you stole from me. You're the height of chivalry." Rolling her eyes, Lucy waved a goodbye and headed in the opposite direction.

Carter took in her lithe figure, the way her slim hips swayed as she walked. Her hair was the color of autumn, he realized: golden tinged with red. It was such a ridiculously maudlin thought that he snorted. *She'd tear your eyes out before she'd let you touch her anyway.*

Carter wandered downtown for a while before he finally ended up near one of the cliffs that overlooked the water. Waves lapped against the shore far below while seagulls screeched and dove into the water. A boat sat in the water not far off from the cliffs' edge, most likely a fisherman.

No one else was around; the silence enveloped him, forcing thoughts to the surface that he'd prefer to bury deep underground.

The day that he'd injured his shoulder was branded into his memory forever. He was one of the best pitchers in the league. With a throw of ninety-eight to one hundred miles per hour, there were few who could manage to hit a ball with him throwing. But Carter had always wanted to be better, faster, stronger. He hadn't been able to surpass one hundred miles per hour, and it drove him insane.

It didn't help when a newbie pitcher drafted into the Los Angeles Bears made the news when he'd thrown faster than

Carter ever had. Carter began to practice harder than ever before. His trainer had cautioned him that he would hurt himself if he didn't let up, but Carter hadn't listened.

He wished he'd listened. Christ, he'd been so fucking stupid.

It had been at practice. Carter had thrown multiple pitches at his average speed, over and over and over. Frustrated over the article about the damn Bears pitcher, Carter threw what would end up being his last real pitch.

He remembered the popping sound the most, even more than the searing pain. He'd thrown that damn ball with all of his strength—and then a pop, a tear, and so much pain that he'd fallen to his knees in agony.

Carter rubbed his aching right shoulder. It always ached these days, especially when it was damp. Ironic, given that he lived in one of the dampest regions in the United States.

He'd done as his orthopedic surgeon had told him and had let his shoulder heal. He'd taken it slowly with physical therapy. He'd played by the rules for a year, but during his last checkup, his surgeon had shaken his head and told him that it wasn't looking good for his return.

I'm giving it another few months. We'll see how you keep healing. But I doubt you'll be able to throw like you used to.

Those words haunted Carter. His career, his livelihood, everything—over in the blink of an eye. Over because he'd been arrogant and pigheaded and had thought he was invincible.

A burst of anger made him pick up a rock and throw it into the water. But since it was using his left arm, it wasn't nearly as satisfying as he'd hoped. He threw a few more and felt slightly better. But then his right shoulder started aching more, reminding him that if he wasn't careful, he'd end up right back where he'd been a year ago.

CARTER NURSED his third beer of the night. It was the only way he was going to get through this cast party, where Hayden Masterson was the main attraction. The entire cast and crew were gathered around him like he was the second coming of Christ. He was surprised no one was drooling or weeping at the actor's feet. Then again, the night was young. He'd give it an hour before someone burst into tears.

If Carter was honest, his eyes weren't so much on Hayden but the little spitfire hanging on his every word. Lucy Younger wore a little black dress that somehow managed to be both modest and sexy at the same time. It showed off her toned arms and legs, and the black set off the creamy paleness of her skin. A light blush colored her cheeks, and when Hayden said something, she threw her head back and laughed.

Another actress said something that made everyone laugh again. Lucy was the one standing the closest to Hayden, her head tilted back as she drank in his every word. When Hayden touched her arm and leaned down to whisper something in her ear, Carter only realized a moment later he was clutching his drink so hard he was liable to shatter the glass.

He didn't care who Lucy or Hayden slept with. He didn't care if Hayden worked his way through every woman on this movie. Carter hadn't come here to sleep around, mostly because he'd gotten bored with the one-night stands and the inevitable mornings where his date for that night would try to stay longer and he'd have to charm them into leaving.

Lately, though, the women knew he wasn't in it for anything but a night. Maybe two nights, if he needed the distraction. His last escapade had ended when his date had orgasmed, then she'd kissed him quickly and gotten dressed. She'd left as soon as she'd arrived. Carter hadn't been sure whether he should've been relieved or annoyed at how quickly she'd bounced.

He finished off his beer and was about to get another when his least favorite person sidled up to him. Jim had somehow managed to tame his hair tonight, but after each drink, it seemed to get bigger and bigger. By the end of the night, Jim would probably look like Albert Einstein after a bender.

"Look at him," said Jim. "I don't know how he does it. He comes into the room and everyone notices."

Carter didn't need to ask who "him" was. "Huh," he grunted.

"It took fucking forever to get his damn agent to agree to the contract. He wanted more and more money, even though this isn't some huge Hollywood project. The budget is good, but it's not huge. You should've seen his list of demands for his trailer: bottled water from the Alps at an exact forty degrees, no warmer or colder. He has to have organic açai shakes every morning along with platters of some other shit I'd never even heard of. It was ridiculous." Jim sighed happily. "But we got him."

Carter was tempted to remind Jim that Carter was a huge baseball star and had been famous way before Hayden Masterson, but he refrained. It wasn't worth antagonizing the man—at least not right now. Maybe tomorrow, when Carter was feeling up to it. Besides, he'd used up most of his Antagonizing Other People Energy on Lucy. He needed to recharge those batteries or he'd end up being a nice guy or something.

Speaking of Lucy—she giggled at something Hayden said. Carter caught Hayden sneaking glances at Lucy's cleavage and he wanted to punch the guy in the face. He could at least be subtle about checking her out. Then again, Lucy seemed to be reveling in the actor's attention. Carter wouldn't be surprised if Hayden took her back to his place that night and fucked her from here to Sunday.

The thought of Hayden's hands on the little spitfire made Carter want to punch him even more than he usually did. It was stupid, considering that Lucy wasn't his in any sense of the word. The only thing she was to him was a woman he enjoyed baiting.

Sure, he found her attractive—those green eyes that reminded him of a cat's; the way she blushed when she was irritated; how she tried to seem tall when she was small enough that Carter could probably fit her into his duffel bag. Not that he was into shoving women into duffel bags—God, he needed to stop drinking. His mind was thinking about weird shit.

"He's going to make this movie big. Maybe bigger than any of us could've imagined." Jim leaned against the wall and sighed again. "Hayden Masterson. I can't believe it."

Carter shot Jim an ironic glance. "He's not a guarantee the movie will do well, though."

"He's pretty good fucking insurance. Nobody else in this movie has his draw."

Hayden moved toward the bar, Lucy following him. They'd rented out the one nice bar here on Hazel Island for the cast party, although compared to the parties Carter had attended during his career, this was practically like having a get-together in someone's basement. The most expensive liquor was probably some shit from Portland. No bottles of Macallan Scotch whiskey, Carter's particular favorite, that cost over seventy-five thousand for a single bottle. Carter was pretty sure the beer he'd been drinking had been bought on sale at Costco.

Lucy had sat down next to Hayden at the bar, her dress inching up her creamy thighs. Hayden was all wide-toothed smiles, and he gestured at the bartender to bring Lucy another drink. Was he going to get Lucy drunk before he took her back to his place? Carter gritted his teeth. What a slimy asshole he was.

Carter looked away from the scene. It was none of his business. He was here to—what, work? When he'd asked Anthony what he'd actually be doing on this movie, Anthony had been vague. *Make sure things don't go to shit. Make sure the producers and writers don't fuck things up. Make sure things stay on budget.*

Carter had looked over the documents Anthony had sent him regarding the budget and scheduling, making notes where necessary. He wasn't remotely qualified for this job, but Anthony hadn't seemed overly concerned with that little detail. If Anthony didn't care, then neither did Carter. Anthony had seemed more interested in giving Carter something to do that didn't involve partying, drinking, or sleeping around.

Jim had left Carter's side to talk to some other poor sucker about how much he loved Hayden Masterson. Carter watched in amusement as Jim interrupted Hayden and Lucy's tête-à-tête at the bar.

Soon other cast members, including a leggy blonde, moved toward the bar. Hayden's attention turned to the blonde, who was not at all subtle about throwing herself at him. Lucy, for her part, attempted to get his attention again, but she'd already been forgotten.

Lucy's gaze collided with Carter's. Instead of looking away, she lifted her chin in defiance. Carter chuckled. He raised his glass to her in a salute. She scowled and went to a table in the corner to talk with one of her castmates.

Carter considered going back to the bed-and-breakfast, but he decided he'd prefer another beer. If he was going to act like he gave a shit about this movie or Hayden or anything in his life that wasn't baseball, he'd need a lot more alcohol in him.

CHAPTER FIVE

Lucy watched as one of the extras—Meredith? Marianne?—slid her hand up Hayden's arms and batted her fake eyelashes. Not that Lucy had anything against fake eyelashes, but this M-named woman looked so fake overall that the eyelashes were the cherry on top.

"If you glare any harder, you're going to singe a hole in her arm," said Erin.

"I'm not glaring."

"Okay. Staring, gazing upon. Whatever term you wanna use, babe. But don't be *too* obvious."

Lucy forced herself to turn her head so she could no longer see what Hayden was doing. She'd thought they were connecting earlier. But then Hayden had gotten distracted. Lucy couldn't compete against multiple other women vying for his attention, not unless she did something crazy, like flash him.

She wasn't yet so desperate as to show him her breasts in public, thank God. The green snake of jealousy still slithered around inside her, especially when she heard Hayden laugh.

"Didn't you think there's something between us?" said Lucy. "He was talking to me most of all tonight."

Erin stirred her drink. "He did seem interested in you," she conceded, "but you're also a beautiful woman. Everyone knows Hayden Masterson loves his pretty ladies."

"I'm more than that, though. We were talking about our favorite movies. His favorite actor is Al Pacino. He told me he's seen *Scarface* at least fifty times; he has almost the whole movie memorized."

Erin wrinkled her nose. "*Scarface*? Isn't that every guy's favorite movie besides *Fight Club*?"

Lucy stuck her tongue out at her friend. Okay, his favorite movie choice wasn't all that inspiring, but Lucy didn't care. She wanted him to turn his attention back to her. She wanted to keep talking about movies and acting and scripts and whether Stanislavski or Meisner had had the right idea when it came to acting methods. She wanted him to gaze down at her with those golden eyes that made her shiver.

"Don't you get it?" whispered Lucy as she once again turned to look at Hayden. "He's…amazing."

Erin let out a low groan, which Lucy pointedly ignored. Her drink empty, she rose to get another and to divert Hayden away from that fake leggy blonde.

Right as Lucy approached, Hayden stood, his arm around the blonde. Before Lucy could react, Hayden and the blonde walked out of the bar, a car's engine signaling that they were most likely not coming back.

Lucy felt like she'd swallowed a rock. *It doesn't mean anything. He hasn't gotten to know you yet.* She'd known Hayden was a player. Well, she couldn't judge him for that. Not that she was a player—she'd had three boyfriends since high school—but she understood why someone would be. Fame was a lonely thing: you were surrounded by people, yet who could you trust?

Lucy reassured herself with those thoughts, but they didn't make her feel much better. Getting another drink, she wandered to a back hallway, which was blessedly quiet. She leaned against the wall and sighed.

"You know, guys like Hayden aren't into women throwing themselves at him," said a voice in the shadows. A voice that seemed intent on following Lucy everywhere she went.

This time, she wasn't even surprised: merely irritated. And embarrassed that he'd been paying attention to her attempt at flirting with Hayden.

"Did I ask for your opinion?" she said. She scowled. "Where are you, anyway? Why are you standing in the dark?"

Carter emerged from the shadows, a beer in his hand. "I could ask you the same question."

"I needed a breather. It's loud in there."

It was strange, but the dim light seemed to make Carter taller, almost intimidating. Then again, he didn't have his usual smirk on his face. He was all stoicism, his brow furrowed as he leaned against the opposite wall from Lucy and crossed his arms.

"Did he go home with her?" he said quietly.

Lucy stilled, the hairs on the back of her neck lifting. She didn't answer for a long moment, struggling against the desire to toss her drink into his face. But suddenly the fight went out of her as she remembered Hayden putting his arm around the leggy blonde.

"He's not home here," she said lamely. "But they did leave

together, if that's what you're wondering. Why? Do you like her?"

"I don't even know her name."

Lucy snorted. "Does it matter?"

"What a cynical girl you are."

She rubbed a finger against the condensation on her glass. "What did you mean? About men like Hayden?"

"Exactly what I said. Men like him want to chase a woman. A woman who makes things easy is boring."

Lucy bristled. "I'm not *easy*."

To her surprise, Carter seemed embarrassed. "I didn't mean—I just meant men like to chase a woman for a little bit. It's an instinctual thing."

Lucy's head started hurting. Mostly, she was confused. "Are you giving me advice?"

Carter finally smiled, but it had a tinge of bitterness to it. "Am I? I guess so."

He stood up from the wall and moved closer to Lucy. Now she could smell the remnants of his cologne, and now that he was closer to one of the lights overhead, she could make out the stubble on his cheeks and jaw.

She looked away. She didn't need to think about Carter as a man. He was a jerk—nothing more, nothing less.

"You want my advice?" he said quietly. "Make Hayden work for it. You're too obvious around him."

"I am not obvious!"

"Little spitfire, everyone in the bar could see your googly eyes for that guy. It was rather nauseating, in an adorable kind of way. Kind of like how a puppy idolizes its master. Sweet, adorable—but not alluring."

Lucy hissed out a breath. She had the sudden urge to push

Carter away from her, but he was so much taller and bigger than her that it would be like a fly pushing at an elephant. Annoying for the elephant, pointless for the fly.

"You know what you should do?" said Carter, despite Lucy's lack of reply.

He tipped back his beer and swallowed. Lucy couldn't help but watch the muscles in his throat, the way his Adam's apple bobbed. Something hot and heavy pooled in her belly.

"You need to make Hayden jealous. Men can't stand when they can't have something—or someone. Right now, you're too available. You're easy. No, don't get your feathers ruffled. You know what I mean." Carter put his hand on the wall above Lucy's head, effectively caging her in. She couldn't look away from the intensity in his gaze.

"What are you saying?" she whispered.

"Be my girlfriend. Then watch Hayden fall at your feet."

Lucy wondered if she was hallucinating from too much alcohol. She blinked, then blinked again, but Carter still stood over her, serious as ever.

"Are you drunk?" she said. "You are. You're messing with me because you think I'm stupid and *easy*—"

"I'm not drunk." He looked at his empty glass. "Okay, I might be a bit buzzed. But that's it. I'm in my right mind."

"Do you have a 'right' mind?"

"Touché. But you didn't answer my question. Let's date. Make a show of things. You're an actress, so it should be easy."

Lucy couldn't breathe. Ducking under his arm, she darted down the hallway. Carter, of course, followed her.

"Why would you want to do this? What's in it for you?" she said.

"The goodness of my heart? Wanting to see true love find its course?" He shrugged. "Does it matter?"

"Yeah, it kind of does."

His lips quirked in that smile that drove her insane. He lifted her chin, his touch gentle but inexorable. "You're right: I don't care about charity."

"What do you care about?" Her voice was breathless, her heart pounding.

His finger trailed down her throat until he pulled away. She told herself she wasn't disappointed by it.

"How about we make this into a bet between each other?"

"What would I win?"

"Hayden, of course. Isn't that what you want most?" His tone was mocking. "But I won't lose. Because there's no way you'll choose Hayden over me." He pressed closer until Lucy was forced against the wall. Only a finger's breadth kept them apart. "You'll tell yourself none of this is real, that it's all a play. But soon you won't be able to tell what's real and what's not. And when I kiss you, you'll only want me to keep doing it, Hayden be damned."

"You're insane," she whispered.

"Probably."

They gazed at each other until Lucy was certain the temperature in the hallway had increased by several degrees. She couldn't help but look at his mouth, wondering what it would be liked to be kissed by this egotistical, cocky asshole.

She shouldn't, she knew. If Anthony and Thea found out… but why would they? They were in Seattle and had their own company to run. And it wasn't like Lucy wasn't an adult who could make her own decisions.

"What's going on in that mind of yours?" said Carter.

"What if Anthony finds out?" She said the words before she could think of a reason why she shouldn't.

Carter frowned. "What if he does? Is he somebody to you?"

Lucy shivered inwardly at the edge in Carter's voice. "It's just that he's dating my sister Thea."

Carter stared at her for a long moment until he let out an incredulous laugh. "Anthony is dating *your* sister? Fuck me. I should've known." He peered at her, as if he were seeing her in a new light. "I see the resemblance. You look just like her." He added in a lower voice, "Let them think what they want. You're a big girl, aren't you?"

Lucy stiffened her spine. He was right, damn him. Thea and Anthony could say whatever they wanted; she wasn't beholden to them. And she wasn't about to let the gauntlet Carter had thrown down be ignored.

"You're wrong. I won't fall for you, because I'm stronger than you think. Besides, why would I fall for a guy who I hate with every fiber of my being?" she said.

"So then what do you have to lose?"

It was crazy, insane, it would end badly, it couldn't work—every excuse that fluttered into Lucy's brain tried to get her to say no. To walk away, go back to the bed-and-breakfast, and never think of this bizarre conversation ever again.

But Lucy hadn't gotten where she was in life without taking some insane risks. What was one more?

"Fine," she said. "Then we have a deal."

Carter's eyebrows rose, as if he were surprised. Then he stepped away and put out his hand. "Deal."

She shook his hand, ignoring how the slide of his palm

against hers made her heart flutter. She imagined silk sheets, kisses down her torso, his hands gliding across her skin.

"We're not sleeping together, just so you know," she blurted.

He smiled. "You keep telling yourself that, little spitfire, if it makes you feel safe at night."

Carter didn't know what time it was when he fell into his bed that night. He was drunk, and he had one particular little spitfire on his mind that made practical matters seem pointless. What did it matter if it was two in the morning and he had to be up by eight o'clock?

He could feel the softness of Lucy's skin even now. He wondered if she was lying in her own bed, staring up at the ceiling, wondering what the hell she'd gotten herself into.

He chuckled. His head spun a little. His bottom lip was numb. That was never a good sign of sobriety. But at the moment, he didn't give two shits that he'd have a nice hangover in a few hours.

Carter fell asleep on top of his comforter. That was when the dreams came.

The dreams had begun to leave him alone, but this particular one was always the same. He was in the Orcas' stadium, practicing his pitch. Sweat beaded on his forehead, and the smell of dirt and turf anchored him. His muscles ached; his shoulder smarted. But that meant he was doing something right. He'd been pushing his body for years, and it had always paid off.

Carter lifted his right arm and threw. The number on the

board: ninety-nine miles per hour. He'd thrown one hundred miles per hour three times today, but he hadn't been that fast in the last five throws.

What do you think about Takahashi throwing 103?

He's coming for your spot, isn't he, Carter?

Fuck Takahashi, thought Carter. He wasn't going to let some newbie eclipse him—even if he was on another team. Even if Carter had been chosen as MVP twice already. He could always be better.

What's wrong with you? Don't be a pussy. I didn't raise my son to give up when things got fucking hard.

Carter always heard his father's voice in his head. Mike Roberts had loved alcohol almost as much as he'd loved baseball—almost, but not quite. When Carter had shown promise as a kid, Mike had been the one who'd pushed Carter every step of the way.

Mike had yelled at Carter's coaches when they hadn't lived up to Mike's impossible standards. He'd drunk entire six-packs of beers as he'd sat in the stands, yelling at Carter to get his ass in gear. Carter couldn't remember how many times his father had been asked to leave Carter's Little League games for being disruptive, sometimes to the point of making other kids cry.

Carter, though, he never cried. He hadn't cried since he'd been five years old.

Carter had made a name for himself, even as a kid. He'd gone to college on a baseball scholarship, playing college ball, then the minor leagues, until he'd been drafted by the major leagues and played for New York before being traded to the Seattle Orcas two years ago.

But now Carter's position was threatened. He wasn't

throwing like he used to due to tendonitis in his shoulder. He'd gone to rehab; he'd worked with a trainer for months. The injury wasn't severe, but it was enough to literally throw him off his game.

Carter threw again: ninety-seven. He scowled, anger building inside him. He hated this feeling, that he was losing control of his own fucking life.

Man up, Carter. Get it the fuck together. Carter kept hearing his father's words in his head, over and over again, like a messed-up mantra.

You aren't anything without baseball. You're not smart. This is your one chance to make something of yourself.

And Carter could feel his career slipping away.

Pissed off and tired, Carter threw one last time that day. He threw harder than he ever had, and his already injured shoulder couldn't take the strain. Carter heard the snap before the pain slammed into him.

Carter awoke with a gasp, covered in a cold sweat. His shoulder ached, as if he'd really been pitching in his dream. Sitting up, he put his head in his hands, nausea roiling through him.

Light leaked through the curtains. How long had he slept? Based on the headache pounding in his temples, it had been long enough for the buzz of alcohol to wear off.

Carter stumbled to the bathroom and showered until the water began to turn cold. After taking some painkillers and drinking an entire bottle of water, he felt a little better. But the dream still clung to him like a vine, wrapping around him until it was like his heart was in a vise.

He leaned over the bathroom counter and took in deep

breaths. "Just a dream, just a dream," he muttered over and over.

He hadn't had that particular dream in a few weeks. He didn't know what would've brought it back like this. Then again, he should've known drinking like that last night would have consequences.

Consequences—shit, *Lucy*. He groaned. Had he really… what? Propositioned her? Except it would be for a *fake* relationship, so he wouldn't be getting anything out of it if Lucy had her way.

He was an idiot, but he couldn't stop the laugh that bubbled in his throat. *In vino veritas*, indeed. He'd been pissed, watching Lucy throw herself at Hayden Masterson, and Carter had decided the next best thing was to help her make Hayden jealous.

Yes, that made perfect sense. It had when he'd been hazy with alcohol, at least.

Should he tell her the deal was off? But he pushed that thought aside. Besides, he was confident that after Lucy had spent time with him, she'd forget all about Hayden. Carter wasn't a famous playboy for nothing, and he would love to watch Hayden Masterson squirm with jealousy.

It was time for revenge, and Carter was more than ready to win this game.

CHAPTER SIX

"Why did you come here?" said Lucy. "You said you wouldn't."

"I never made any promise like that." Hayden looked away, his expression rueful. "Did you think I could stay away from you, Miranda?"

It was their first rehearsal together in Hayden's trailer, and they'd been working on this particular scene all morning. Hayden preferred to play Gabriel as stoic, almost emotionless, but Lucy could feel the brimming emotion underneath. It was a testament to Hayden's skill that he could imbue every word of the script with such feeling.

Lucy/Miranda stepped toward a table. She traced a figure eight on the tabletop before picking up the discarded ring. "I don't need this anymore," she whispered.

"Wait," said Hayden, ending the scene. "Shouldn't Miranda be angrier in this scene? Gabriel did cheat on her, right?"

"I think it's more complicated than that. She *is* angry with him, but there's still love there, too. She's torn between two different emotions. She wants to hate the man she still loves."

Hayden peered at her, assessing her. Lucy wondered if she'd overstepped: Hayden was the bigger actor, after all. He was the one with the Oscar nomination; she was a nobody in the grand scheme of things.

Hayden tapped the script. "Maybe not angry to the point that she's throwing things at his head, but you made the line sound hesitant. She should be more forceful."

Irritation nipped at Lucy: Miranda was her role, not his. But she pushed the irritation aside. Hayden Masterson knew how to act, and Lucy would be stupid to ignore his critiques.

They played the scene again, this time Lucy putting more anger into her lines. It wasn't hard to do. She thought about Carter Roberts and his stupid, smirking face, and the anger was right in front of her.

Although at the moment, she was angrier at herself than at Carter. Why had she agreed to be Carter's fake girlfriend last night? She hadn't drunk that much alcohol. It must have been a moment of pure insanity.

"Let's take a break. I need to make a phone call anyway," said Hayden an hour before they were to start filming. "You good?" He touched Lucy's shoulder, smiling down at her.

Her heart flip-flopped in her chest. Then she remembered that Hayden had left with another woman last night.

Her smile froze on her face. "I'm good," she stammered.

"When I heard who my leading lady would be, I was kind of skeptical."

Lucy raised an eyebrow. "And now?"

"You've convinced me that you're more than up to the challenge."

She blushed, feeling giddy. *This is the guy you've had a crush on for a year*, she reminded herself. *Don't let anyone else distract you from what you want.*

"Can I tell you a secret?" she said.

"A secret? Now I'm intrigued."

Lucy had wanted to tell Hayden that they'd already met once before at Julia Hendricks's home last year. Julia was another actress who'd starred in a film with Hayden two years ago. Lucy had only gotten an invitation after she'd begged her agent to pull some strings.

"Do you remember the party at Julia Hendricks's place? The one last July?"

Hayden tilted his head to the side. "Julia has tons of parties. I'm pretty sure I went to at least four in July alone."

"Um, it was a really big party." Lucy searched her memories for some specific detail. "Justin Bieber was supposed to come, but he apparently bailed last minute. Julia wasn't happy about it since she'd promised her niece Justin would be there."

"Oh, *that* party. I do remember—vaguely." Hayden shrugged, smiling. "I go to a lot of parties, you know."

"We met at that party." When Hayden gave her a blank look, she added hurriedly, "It was for, like, a minute. I wouldn't expect you to remember me."

Hayden peered at her like he had earlier, as if he didn't recognize her in that moment. Then he shook his head. "I'm sorry. I don't remember you, but like you said, if it was just for a minute, I was probably distracted. And possibly drunk." He chuckled, but it sounded hollow—almost forced.

Lucy's shoulders slumped. It was stupid to be disappointed, but she'd foolishly dreamed of the day she'd meet Hayden again. He'd tell her that she'd captivated him that night, that he hadn't stopped thinking about her. That their meeting now must be fate.

"I remembered you," she said shyly. She looked up at him through her lashes. "I couldn't believe I'd gotten the chance to meet you."

"And now here we are, working together. What a coincidence. I had a nice time last night, until we were interrupted, though. I wanted to hear more about your thoughts on Stanislavski."

"You didn't seem too annoyed by the interruption," she pointed out.

"Who, Meredith?" Hayden shrugged. "If it makes you feel better, nothing happened. She wanted to pick my brain about another upcoming project I'm doing and if there was any way she could get a role." His teeth flashed as he smiled. "Were you jealous?"

"No, of course not."

And strangely enough, Lucy hadn't thought once about Hayden and Meredith after her conversation with Carter. The way he'd touched her and the way his voice had stroked places inside her she didn't want to name had kept her up last night. She'd forgotten that she was supposed to be jealous over Hayden taking another woman back to his room.

Carter is a jerk who just wants to mess with you. Hayden is the one that you want. Don't get confused, she told herself sternly.

Hayden's phone rang in his pocket. "As much as I'd like to continue this conversation, this can't wait."

Hayden excused himself, and Lucy left his trailer to go for a walk until filming started. She needed to clear her head. She must still be hungover to keep thinking about Carter like this.

"Even when he's not here, he's driving me crazy," she

muttered to herself. She kicked at pieces of gravel as she walked, imagining that they were Carter's head.

Lucy's stomach rumbled, but she didn't want to eat anything. Whenever she got anxious, her appetite disappeared. Once she'd lost ten pounds in two weeks, which, given the fact that she was already tiny, had made her look emaciated. Her agent had been so concerned that she'd taken Lucy straight to the nearest fast-food restaurant and told her to eat her weight in French fries.

When Lucy saw Carter sitting on the steps to his trailer, she couldn't be surprised. The man seemed to follow her everywhere.

"Shouldn't you be working?" she said, approaching him. With him sitting on the bottom step and her standing, she could look him in the eye.

He raised an eyebrow. "Are you my boss now?"

"Do you *have* a boss?"

"Sure I do." Carter thought for a long moment. "Well, not really. I *am* the boss. And in case you were wondering, I already did what I needed to do this morning." He bit into a bright red apple, chewing it with relish before swallowing. "Did you need something?"

Based on his reaction, maybe he didn't remember what had happened last night. She prayed he'd been too drunk to remember, because otherwise, this was going to be the most awkward conversation ever.

"You look like you're going to throw up," he said lightly. "Sit down before you faint."

"I never faint," she grumbled, but she did sit down. She also made certain to keep at least a foot of space between them.

"You seem like you want something." He took another bite of his apple. "But despite what you might think, I can't read a woman's mind."

God, he was irritating. Lucy stretched out her legs and said, "Do you remember what you said to me last night?"

His eyes flashed with amusement. "Of course, little spit-fire. Are you here to renege? Because I didn't take you for a quitter."

Lucy scowled. "I never should have agreed to it. It's crazy and stupid, being your fake girlfriend. Besides, Hayden—" She stopped when she saw the dark look cross over Carter's face.

He took another large bite of his apple before tossing the core into a nearby trash can, the sound making Lucy flinch.

"He went home with another woman," said Carter in scathing tones. "He didn't even think about you after he saw her. Is that what you want?"

"He said nothing happened between them."

Carter laughed. "And you believed him? I thought you were smart, babe. You have to be, in this business."

An angry flush crawled up Lucy's cheeks. Getting up, she stood over him, mostly because sitting next to him made them seem too cozy together.

"You don't know him. He's been nothing but a gentle-man," she said.

"That means he thinks of you like a sister."

"He told me he thought I was pretty."

"That's it?" Carter snorted. "I knew he was an idiot, but he must be as dumb as a sack of rocks. A real man would've told you that you're beautiful. That you intoxicate him with every movement. That your voice is like a drug every time you say so much as 'yes' or 'no.'"

Lucy couldn't swallow past the lump in her throat. "Is that what you think of me?" she whispered.

Carter tapped her nose. "No, spitfire. Of course not. This is just an act, remember?"

Humiliation washed through Lucy. "What does it matter to you anyway, if Hayden wants me or not? You and I, we're not dating. You don't even like me."

To her dismay, he stood up, lording his height over her. She wished he weren't so handsome, so masculine. It'd be easier if she didn't feel her heart turn over in her chest every time he came near her.

"I don't care," he said. "But we had a bet. If you renege, that means I win. And we both know you don't want that."

"You wouldn't win anything beyond thinking that you won. That makes no sense."

"But that would be enough. You'd hate it, knowing that I'd scared you away, that you were so attracted to me that you knew within a day of spending time with me, you'd forget all about that guy."

Lucy couldn't draw enough air into her lungs. The world had shrunk until it was only she and Carter. She had the sudden insane desire to kiss him, if only to prove that she wasn't attracted to him. Not in the slightest.

She wanted Hayden. She knew that—but why did her body tell her otherwise? When Hayden had touched her, there hadn't been this crackling chemistry between them.

"You sound like you do care," she accused, trying to figure out what was up and what was down.

Carter smirked. "You keep telling yourself that, little

spitfire. Now, are we on or not? Because your Prince Charming is coming around the corner, so it's now or never."

Lucy refused to let Carter win. She would prove to him that he couldn't get into her pants so easily. She didn't care that he was handsome or that he had stupid dimples when he smiled or that he smelled like cedar and spice.

She grabbed his hand and entwined their fingers. Then she tipped her head back and laughed, like he'd said something hilarious.

"There you go," he whispered. He put his arm around her, pulling her close, and he leaned down to whisper in her ear, "He's watching us. Put on a good show for him."

As an actress, Lucy knew how to perform. She knew how to embody a character, let emotions flow through her, let some made-up story influence her body and her voice. This was just another role.

She told herself that, but when she tipped her head back and gazed into Carter's eyes, she wasn't sure of anything. She wasn't even sure of her own name right then.

"Lucy?" said Hayden over her shoulder. "It's about time for filming to start."

She almost pushed Carter away, but he gripped her hand tighter. "She'll be right there," answered Carter. "Won't you, sweetheart?"

Lucy wished she could see Hayden's face. Was he jealous? "Yes, I'll be right there," she repeated.

"We don't have much time. You don't want to be late." Hayden sounded insistent now.

Lucy turned so she could face Hayden. He didn't look jealous so much as confused.

"I didn't know you two were dating," said Hayden, eyeing them both. "I thought you preferred tall girls, Carter."

Lucy stiffened, but Carter laughed. "I like anything pretty and female. Just like you."

Something dangerous swirled in the air between these two, and Lucy had a feeling she was going to get caught in the middle of the storm if she wasn't very careful.

Carter caressed her back. "You should get to set. You know how Jim hates when people are late, like Hayden said."

Before Lucy could react, Carter dipped his head and kissed her. It was a quick kiss, but it shot heat down to Lucy's bones. His stubble brushed her cheek; his lips were firm yet unbearably soft. When Carter pulled away, she wanted to bring his head back down and make him really kiss her.

"I have to go," she whispered.

"Yes, you do." Carter almost sounded sad.

Lucy didn't know how she managed to walk to set without her knees giving way. She didn't know what to say to Hayden, and she honestly didn't much care about talking to him. She could only feel that kiss from Carter.

What the hell had she gotten herself into now? was her only thought for the rest of the afternoon.

CHAPTER SEVEN

That evening, Carter felt antsy. He considered going to a bar, maybe finding a willing woman to return to the bed-and-breakfast with him. There had to be bachelorettes on this godforsaken island, right? Ones who were as cynical about life as he was right now.

The thought of taking some stranger back didn't appeal to him, strangely enough. Normally it would have. Feeling out of sorts, Carter decided he'd wander around the island and see what he found.

Hazel Island was only about ten square miles, its one town was named Hazel Town, but nobody called it that. Outside of the town's center, there were houses scattered throughout the island. Some overlooked the cliffs for which the island was famous.

Carter wandered down a street that ran parallel to a large park. It was a few hours before sunset, and families and singles walked up and down the sidewalk. Some turned into the entrance for the park, while others were most likely on their way home.

Nobody stopped Carter for an autograph or a photo this time. He wasn't particularly in the mood to be nice to fans. Usually he enjoyed the attention, even expected it. Tonight, however, he wasn't interested in being pleasant.

During a meeting with Jim and the writers, Carter had had to force himself to stop thinking about that damn kiss with Lucy. He'd had to talk about schedules and budgets until he'd wanted to blow his brains out. He'd called Anthony after the meeting to tell him he'd been an idiot to let him do this.

"Are you quitting?" Anthony had said, sounding more amused than annoyed.

"I want to. Why did I agree to this again?"

"Because I didn't need to keep looking at your sad, mopey face all summer. Maybe you could start enjoying yourself. You're on an island, you know. People like islands."

Carter had given his friend some choice words and had promptly hung up. He had no real reason to be irritated about his gig here: it involved not much work on his part at the end of the day, and it allowed him more freedom than he'd had when he'd been playing.

God, he just wanted to return to baseball. He'd always known that he'd retire eventually—no athlete could play forever. But to stop playing because of a bum shoulder, to have his career cut short…

Carter had wandered into the park, and he stopped short when he reached a baseball field. He blew out a breath. Of course he'd find the baseball field. It was in his blood.

He watched as a father tossed a ball to his son, who didn't look to be older than ten. The boy had on a helmet that made him look like a bobblehead, and he wiggled his butt a little as he held the bat.

Carter smiled, crossing his arms. The boy's dad threw the ball underhand, and the boy managed to hit it hard enough that it would've gotten close to second base if the dad hadn't caught it.

"Right on!" his dad said. "One more time."

The boy got into position. This time, he hit the ball high enough that his dad had to run after it. The boy managed to make a home run. When he got to home base, he high-fived his dad, the two of them laughing.

Something twisted in Carter's chest. The only thing his own father had ever done during practice sessions was tell Carter that he could do better.

Always better, faster, higher. Carter could never measure up to his dad's impossible expectations, but he'd tried. He would try until his shoulder was on fire, until his fingers ached from gripping the ball. He'd throw until he'd simply run out of energy, and his dad would shake his head. *Not gonna get anywhere with that attitude.*

"Hey, can I join you two?" said Carter, jogging up to the father-son duo.

The boy's father blinked in surprise before saying, "Wait? Are you Carter Roberts?"

"Guilty as charged," said Carter.

The boy was staring up at Carter with eyes as wide as an owl's. In a whisper, the boy breathed, "Are you really him?"

"You're his favorite pitcher ever," said the man before he held out his hand. "I'm Steve, and this is Danny. Danny, introduce yourself to Mr. Roberts here."

Danny stuck out his hand, which Carter shook with all of the appropriate solemnity of the occasion.

"It's nice to meet you," said Carter. "I saw you made a home run, too."

"I've watched every game you've been in," said Danny in a rush. "When you pitched and struck out Perry during the World Series…" Danny sighed happily. "I rewatched that so many times."

That had been the moment that had clinched the win for the Orcas, and Carter looked back on that memory with a mixture of fondness and sadness.

"I'm kind of out of practice. You wanna practice with me?" Carter glanced at Steve. "If it's okay with your dad."

Steve agreed readily, not questioning why Carter Roberts of all people wanted to play catch with his ten-year-old son. Maybe he assumed it was some strange quirk of professional players. Or he was being particularly nice to one of his young fans.

As Carter played catch with Danny and provided him with pointers, he relaxed for the first time in what felt like ages. The feeling of a ball in his hand, the leather smell of the mitt (borrowed from Steve who stood on the sidelines watching), the crack of the bat. For a second, Carter felt transported, even if he was just playing with a young kid in the middle of a park. Carter could forget for a moment that his shoulder was possibly beyond repair and that his career had been destroyed during that single moment of madness.

Soon, though, the sun had set enough that there wasn't enough light to keep playing. Danny jogged up to Carter, peppering him with questions. Steve finally told his son they needed to head home.

Carter still held the ball they'd been using. When he tried

to hand it back to Steve, the man said, "Keep it. We have plenty at home."

A few distant streetlamps flickered on, providing a little more light. Carter stood at the pitcher's mound, tossing the ball back and forth between his hands.

He hadn't tried to pitch since his last surgery. His physical therapist had told him he could throw again after six weeks, but obviously not like he used to. He'd have to throw as lightly as Steve had thrown to Danny. Which meant that Carter couldn't throw at all in his estimation.

Carter got into position, pulling his arm back, his muscles still remembering the movement that was imprinted onto his very soul. In a rush of air, he threw, the ball hitting the metal fence a second later.

Lucy wasn't entirely certain why she'd felt the need to follow Carter. She'd been taking a walk on the trail and was about to return to the bed-and-breakfast when she'd caught sight of him.

She inhaled a sharp breath as she watched him pitch. The ball flew so fast that it was a mere blur until it struck the metal fence and thumped onto the ground.

It was dark enough that Lucy could stand in the shadows and watch him without him knowing she was there. But watching him like this and knowing some vague details about his injury and subsequent benching, she felt like she was intruding on something unbearably private.

Yet she couldn't force herself to walk away, either.

He pitched a second time. Lucy caught her breath, in awe

at his speed. No wonder he was so arrogant and self-assured: no normal human could throw like that. That kind of talent was rare and breathtaking.

After his second pitch, Carter didn't immediately jog to pick up the ball for a third pitch. He rubbed his shoulder, wincing.

Lucy's heart squeezed. She shouldn't have come here. She didn't need to feel anything but dislike for this man who'd upended her life in a few days.

She stepped backward to retreat, only to step on a branch that cracked so loudly everyone in a one-mile radius probably heard it. Knowing she was caught, she stepped into the light and approached Carter.

"What are you doing here?" he said.

When he didn't make a joke or snarky aside, Lucy knew he wasn't feeling like himself. He kept rubbing his shoulder and trying to stretch it, his face contorting with pain as he did so.

"Are you okay?" she said softly.

He shrugged. "I'm fine. It'll stop throbbing eventually."

Lucy was tempted to tell him he should go straight back to his room and ice his shoulder, but she wasn't his girlfriend. She was just his fake girlfriend, because she wanted to get Hayden's attention.

"Fuck," muttered Carter. "I shouldn't have thrown that second pitch."

"I've never seen anyone throw as fast as you. I don't know how anyone manages to hit a ball that you throw at them."

Carter's lips lifted in a smile. "That's the thing: they don't." But his smile soon disappeared. "That wasn't fast, at least not for me. It was probably closer to eighty, maybe slower. I used to throw a hundred. Until my goddamn shoulder gave out on me."

"But you'll play again, right? Once you heal?"

His expression was pitying, like she'd asked if unicorns were real. "Little spitfire, a torn rotator cuff is the worst injury a pitcher can get. There's no going back from it."

Seeing the starkness in his gaze, the devastation, made Lucy wonder if this was the first time he'd admitted such a statement to himself. Her heart squeezed for the second time that night.

"But maybe I'll be one of the lucky ones. My surgeon hasn't written me off yet," he said.

"So you have to wait?"

"Yes, wait and see. And, yes, it does suck."

"I'm sorry," she offered, rather lamely. "I know there's nothing I can say to make it better."

"Would you make it better if you could? I thought you didn't like me." His smile returned.

"Just because I don't like someone doesn't mean I want them to suffer. I'm not inhuman. I mean, yes, if you fell down in front of a crowd of people, I'd laugh and say you deserved it, but—"

He held up a hand. "I get you. You don't need to explain your sudden interest in pitying me." He glanced at his watch. "We should get back. Were you here alone?"

"Yes. Why?"

"You shouldn't be in a park by yourself at night."

Lucy put her hands on her hips. "I think this island is pretty safe, Carter. I doubt there are any boogeymen looking to kidnap me."

"But you'd be so easy to kidnap." He stepped closer to her,

smiling down at her. "You're so tiny. I could throw you over my shoulder without any effort."

"I am *not* tiny. I am *petite*. There's a difference. You make it sound like I should be a part of a Polly Pocket or something."

"What the hell is a Polly Pocket?"

Lucy couldn't help but laugh at his face. "You never had a Polly Pocket as a kid? It was this container…thing that was a house inside, and there were tiny figurines that went with it called Polly."

"You're terrible at describing this."

Annoyed, she pulled up a photo of a Polly Pocket on her phone and showed it to him.

Carter smirked. "Darlin'," he drawled, "do I look like the kind of guy who would've played with something like that?"

Lucy blushed, mostly because she started to imagine what he would enjoy playing with. Suddenly their innocuous banter heated up, and only because of the way Carter looked at her. Like he wanted to eat her up in one gulp.

"Did you always want to be a baseball player?" she blurted.

"Yeah, pretty much. It was all I was ever good at, anyway."

"I wanted to be an actress when I was in first grade. I was in this school play, and I loved it. When I found out people got paid to act, I decided that was what I wanted to be."

"And now you're living your dream." He chucked her under the chin. "What a lucky girl you are."

Her hackles rose. "You don't have to be condescending about it. It's not like I haven't worked my ass off to get here, you know."

"You're right," he said soberly, to her surprise. "I never

meant to imply otherwise. If anyone has worked hard, it's you."

She was so stunned by the sudden compliment that words failed her. She didn't understand this man at all. One second he insulted her, the next he said things like that. Her initial impression that he was some smarmy playboy hadn't been remotely correct. There were layers to this man that she wished to uncover, all the while knowing it would most likely result in her own heart breaking.

"I thought about giving it all up," she confessed, feeling like she owed him a piece of herself. "Before I got this role. I was about to pack up my bags and wave the white flag."

Carter didn't say anything, but she knew he was listening.

"My family supports me, but they also worry about me. My older brothers especially. Trent is always calling me to make sure I have enough money because I asked him to help with my rent once." She winced. "Okay, maybe twice. But that was a long time ago."

"He cares about you," said Carter softly.

"I know. They all do. And when I counted up all the bills that were overdue and how my bank account had only a negative balance, I thought, *Maybe Trent's right. Maybe I should go home and get a real job.*" She swallowed past the lump in her throat. "I had dreamed of becoming an actress for so long that I had never considered it might not happen, no matter how hard I tried to make it happen."

"And even if you do make it, it can disappear before you know it."

Lucy closed her eyes for a moment. "Yes. Of course. I'm complaining about nothing."

"No, you're not."

Carter looked away, and Lucy drank in his profile. His jawline was exquisite; she had a feeling her sister, Thea, a graphic artist, would love to draw this man. Lucy wanted to touch him; the desire was so intense she had to put her hands behind her back to keep herself from doing something truly stupid.

They stood in silence for a long moment, the only sounds those of distant cars and the rustling of the trees.

Then Carter said suddenly, "We should go on a date."

Lucy gaped at him.

His normally easy smile returned. "A date. Especially if it's at a place your one true love hangs out at. He needs to see us together."

Strangely, Lucy felt disappointment roll through her. Of course he meant a fake date. He didn't really want to take her out. She probably wasn't his type anyway, given the fact that he had access to any beautiful woman he could possibly want.

"We should," she choked out, glad for once that she was an actress and could make herself sound enthused when she wanted to hide under a rock. "Hayden told me he hangs out at Verity on Wednesdays for their happy hour."

"Excellent." Carter wasn't smiling now. "Put on your best dress, little spitfire. We're gonna make your guy so jealous he won't know what hit him."

CHAPTER EIGHT

The moment Carter saw Lucy step out of her room wearing an emerald cocktail dress that hugged her body, he knew he'd made a huge mistake.

When he didn't say anything, Lucy shuffled her feet. "Something wrong?"

He was tempted to tell her to go back into her room and find something else to wear. Preferably a burlap sack, because dammit, she was too sexy for her own good, wearing a dress like that. That dress could tempt the pope to forsake his vows. The green fabric left little to the imagination, and the sweetheart neckline put the lovely curves of her breasts and shoulders on display.

The dress hit right above the knee, but it certainly showed enough of her legs to tempt a saint. And Carter was no saint to begin with.

And neither is Hayden Masterson.

Scowling inwardly, he finally said, "Let's go, before we're late for our reservation."

When they were seated inside the restaurant—a quaint

71

little Italian place that overlooked the water—Carter felt like he'd gotten a hold of himself. Just because he wanted to throw Lucy over his shoulder and take her straight to bed didn't mean he had to give in to the impulse. Besides, the reason he was doing this was to piss off Hayden and show him what it felt like to have someone else steal a woman right from under your nose.

Lucy ordered a glass of chardonnay while Carter stuck with red wine.

"Is he here?" said Carter softly after their waiter had left.

Lucy frowned. "Is who here?"

"Your Prince Charming."

"Oh." She set her wineglass down, accidentally hitting the side of her bread plate. "Oh, no. I mean, I haven't looked yet."

She peered over Carter's shoulder, which made him chuckle.

"You're going to have to at least try to be subtle," he drawled.

"Oh, hush." Her eyes widened. "He's here—at the bar. And he's alone."

Gritting his teeth, Carter forced himself to put on his laziest grin. "Then we should give him a good show. Lean closer to me. Yeah, like that. Act like I'm talking about the most fascinating thing ever."

Lucy put her chin on her hand and fluttered her eyelashes. Her leaning over only made her breasts push up against her dress. Carter's cock stirred, irritating the hell out of him.

Why did he have to want *this* woman? Despite his assurances to her that she wouldn't be able to resist him, he wasn't so sure she wouldn't drop him like a hot potato if Hayden so much as crooked his finger at her.

Carter took a long drink of his wine, mostly to fortify himself.

"What do you like to do for fun? Besides baseball," said Lucy.

"That's what you're going with? Hobbies?"

"Hey, you weren't coming up with anything, mister."

"Darlin', you should know the answer to that. If I'm not playing, I'm fucking a beautiful woman. Or maybe more than one at a time."

"You can't be fucking women all the time. What about when you're tired or sick? What if you have the flu? Nobody likes to have sex when they have the flu." She smiled innocently.

"I never get sick, so your point is moot."

"Everyone gets sick."

Carter snorted. "I don't."

"You're terrible at this." Lucy leaned back in her chair and sighed. "Okay, I'll tell you something about myself. When I'm not acting, I like to post ads on Craigslist for random hookups, usually involving Jell-O molds and inflatable pool toys."

Carter choked on his wine. Gasping for breath, he said, "Touché, little spitfire. You win."

The smile she gave him was so radiant that it almost stopped his heart. The heart he was pretty sure hadn't existed in a long, long time.

It didn't help that the candlelight brought out the reddish hues in her hair, or that she'd worn red lipstick that made her look even more kissable than usual.

"I'm curious, though," he said, "what do you do with the Jell-O molds?"

Her lips twitched before she leaned closer to whisper, "It's a secret."

That husky whisper went straight to his cock. He was glad he was sitting down, because otherwise, everyone and the waiter would know he was enjoying this fake date way too much.

"A bottle of champagne for the table," said the waiter, "from the gentleman at the bar."

Carter didn't need to ask who the gentleman at the bar was. Before the waiter could uncork the bottle, he snapped, "Take it back. We don't want it."

The waiter barely batted an eyelash. He picked up the two champagne glasses he'd brought and left without another word.

"You didn't have to be rude. Besides, Hayden might think that I didn't want champagne, not you," said Lucy.

"I don't give a damn what he wants. You're on a date with *me*. He can drink the damn bottle himself."

A few minutes of silence passed, only broken up by the waiter bringing them their entrees. Neither of them, however, touched their food. Lucy poked at her salmon; Carter drank another glass of wine.

"I'm sorry, spitfire," he said quietly. "I didn't mean to snap at you."

"I know." She smiled again and, after taking a bite of her salmon, said, "You still haven't answered my question. What do you do for fun besides the obvious?"

Carter considered. When was the last time he'd done

something for the hell of it? Baseball had consumed his life for so long that he didn't know the answer right away.

"I like to read," he said finally.

"Really? Like what?"

"Nonfiction, I guess. I like biographies about American history, the presidents especially."

"Are you going to tell me you're a closet *Hamilton* fan before breaking into song?"

"Fuck, no. I don't do musicals, and I don't sing."

Lucy clucked her tongue. "You can't write off an entire genre. Musicals are amazing. Have you ever actually watched one?"

"I don't need to watch one to know I wouldn't like it."

After that, Lucy tried her best to persuade him to listen to the *Hamilton* soundtrack and to watch *Moulin Rouge* with her, which was her favorite musical of all time. By the end of the evening, Carter had learned about her favorite nonmusical movie (*The Philadelphia Story*), her favorite director (Guillermo del Toro), and her favorite childhood book (*Anne of Green Gables*). Carter had told her his favorite movie (*Fight Club*, which had made her snort-giggle), his favorite director (didn't have one), and his favorite childhood book (he couldn't remember).

Carter became so immersed in their conversation that he forgot all about Hayden and his attempt to interrupt their date. Their fake date, but Hayden didn't know that.

"Did you not like the champagne?" said Hayden as he approached the pair, a wide smile on his face. "Because I could've ordered you two something else."

"Oh, no, we just—"

Carter interrupted Lucy. "I don't need other guys buying my date drinks."

Hayden put his hands up. "Hey, no hard feelings. Just thought I'd be nice, seeing you two here."

Lucy looked like she wanted to run and hide, and irritation burbled inside Carter. In a show of possessiveness, Carter wrapped his arm around Lucy's waist until she pressed against his side. He caught a whiff of her hair—something sweet and fruity—and wanted to bury his hands in her hair and kiss her until she forgot all about Hayden.

"Are you two really together?" said Hayden. "Because it must be a new thing."

"It is. New, that is." Lucy reached behind Carter's back and dug her nails into his palm to keep him quiet. "We just started—doing this."

"Huh." Hayden shot an amused look at Carter. "I didn't think you dated anyone. You're one night and done."

"A guy can change," said Carter. He took hold of Lucy's hand to keep her from swiping her claws at him a second time.

"People don't change that much. At least not for the better." Hayden chuckled.

"You would know," said Carter.

Lucy pulled away from Carter, much to his annoyance. "Thank you for the champagne. Even if we didn't drink it."

"Then we'll have to do this again so you can drink it," said Hayden with a wink.

Watching Lucy, her color high, her attention fully on this smarmy asshole, Carter was liable to punch something. Or preferably, someone.

Just because this was a fake date didn't mean he let other men poach in his territory.

"We need to go." Carter took Lucy's arm. "See you later, Hayden."

Carter didn't wait for Lucy to say goodbye or to hear Hayden's response. He pulled her outside, the night air chilled despite the time of year. When they got some yards away from the restaurant, Lucy wrenched her arm from his grasp.

"What the hell was that all about?" she hissed.

"Are you seriously asking me that? You're *my* date. Not his. He doesn't get to try to lure you away from me without me doing something about it."

"Lure me? Isn't that what you want him to do?" Lucy was agog, shaking her head. "You acted like you were going to beat him up. Or pee on me," she added wryly.

"Don't tempt me."

"You want to pee on me?"

Carter snorted. "Honey, I like kinky shit, but nothing that kinky."

His joke managed to lighten the mood somewhat, and Lucy's ruffled feathers settled down. She rubbed her arms.

"You're cold." Carter wrapped his arms around her, and this time, she didn't resist him.

"What are we doing?" she whispered against his chest. "This has been a terrible idea. I don't know what's what anymore."

"Are you saying you want to call it off?" *Please say no.*

Lucy didn't say anything for such a long moment that Carter tilted her head up so he could look into her eyes.

"Do you want to end it, little spitfire? Because you're going to have to say the words."

Lucy gazed up at him, her eyes wide and such a pretty shade of green that if Carter wrote poetry, he'd pen a sonnet to them. Good thing he was a ballplayer, then. He wasn't about to do something as asinine as write an ode to a woman's eyes.

"You better make up your mind, because Hayden's looking at us right now," said Carter softly.

Lucy stiffened, but she didn't pull away. In fact, she licked her lips, as if anticipating something.

"Carter, this thing—"

He didn't want to hear her protestations. He didn't want to hear why this was stupid, crazy, ridiculous, every adjective listed under *moronic* in the thesaurus.

So he kissed her.

It wasn't a chore to kiss this little spitfire. She was like lightning against his tongue. When she gasped in surprise, he swallowed the sound and deepened the kiss. She fell against him, clutching at his coat lapels. She tasted like wine and gunpowder—and she lit a fire inside of him that he was pretty certain would never go out.

When he slipped his tongue inside her mouth, she shivered. He groaned, his cock so hard now that it was painful. The slide of their tongues and the brush of their mouths made everything else around them disappear. Carter forgot about Hayden, and how this was all for show.

It was all for show—right? Guilt pricked him. He'd started this as a way to get back at Hayden, but it was quickly going in a direction he never could've anticipated.

Lucy sighed, ending the kiss. Her lips were kiss-bruised, her eyes glassy. The only reason Carter didn't take her straight to his bed was…well, he didn't know. He didn't care about the reasons why he shouldn't anymore.

"Is he still there?" said Lucy.

Hayden still stood only a few yards away. When Carter caught Hayden's eyes, Hayden's mouth twisted into a strange semblance of a smile. Then he walked away.

"He's gone," said Carter, not mentioning the weird smile. "I guess the kiss scared him off." Even to his ears, he sounded bitter.

"Oh, okay. Good. Or not good. I don't know." Lucy wrapped her arms around herself, and suddenly what had felt like the most intimate moment in Carter's life had ended with the both of them completely alone.

LUCY SAID nothing on the drive back to the bed-and-breakfast. She didn't know what to say.

That kiss—it had devastated her. She'd never been kissed like that in her entire life. And throughout this whole evening, she hadn't been thinking about Hayden: her mind had been solely on Carter. Getting to know him, seeing him laugh, watching in confusion as he acted possessive one moment and then pushed her away the next. When he'd kissed her and Hayden had been watching, it had been so hot that her body still hummed from the sensations.

"Good night," said Carter as he dropped her off at her door.

Before he turned to go, Lucy blurted, "Thank you. For tonight." She shoved her hands in her coat pockets. "I had a nice time."

"Well, you did what you needed to do. Hayden was there and he wanted to take you all for himself. Men hate knowing they can't have something."

Lucy flushed to the roots of her hair. She hadn't meant that at all, but of course Carter would assume she was pleased about this development. She *should* be pleased. Hayden had tried to buy her a bottle of champagne to interrupt their date, for God's sake. Men didn't do that unless they wanted a woman for their own.

She deflated, feeling foolish. "Yeah, I guess. It was good. He seemed interested."

"He'll be yours for the taking soon enough."

Lucy had the inexplicable urge to cry. She wanted Carter to put his arms around her again and kiss her. Her body came to life anytime he so much as looked at her.

But she wanted Hayden. She'd been into him for a year; she'd dreamed of the day she could meet him again and catch his interest. They had everything in common. She and Carter were so different that Lucy knew nothing good could come of their relationship.

Relationship? They had no relationship. Lucy bit her tongue to stifle hysterical laughter.

"Good night, little spitfire," said Carter, breaking Lucy's train of thought.

"Good night."

He grinned. "Try not to dream of me, but I know you will."

Lucy didn't even try to deny the statement. She hurried inside her room, locking the door behind her, knowing that it wouldn't keep this pulsing desire for Carter at bay.

CHAPTER NINE

That weekend, Lucy had the afternoon off from filming, as the crew was currently filming scenes that only involved Hayden. Gwen had invited Lucy to go to the beach with her and two other friends, and Lucy had accepted without hesitation.

It was a brilliant, cloudless day, and everyone on the island seemed to be on the beach this afternoon. Wearing her favorite dark blue bikini, Lucy lay on a blanket and soaked in the sun. Despite living in Los Angeles, she hadn't gotten a tan in ages since she was always busy working.

"Lucy, I want you to meet someone. Or someones, really," said Gwen.

Lucy opened her eyes to see two women sitting down on Gwen's blanket, one of whom had brought a beach chair with her. One woman was a curvy brunette with olive skin and wore a vintage red one-piece; the other was a pale, tall blonde, her swimsuit a demure black. When the blonde turned her head to get something out of her bag, Lucy noticed that she had what looked like a birthmark on her face.

"Lucy, this is Alex," said Gwen, pointing to the brunette, "and this is Felicity. Alex owns the bookstore, and Felicity freelances." Gwen smiled, pushing her heavy red hair over her shoulder. "Felicity actually won't tell us what she does. She's mysterious."

Felicity smiled but didn't say anything to contradict Gwen's assertion.

"Freelance? Like write? Or graphic design?" said Lucy, intrigued.

"She won't tell you," said Alex as she opened a bottle of beer. "All she'll tell us is that she writes. I think she's some famous writer but hides away because her fans would mob her."

Felicity shook her head. "I'm not famous." Her voice was so soft that Lucy almost didn't hear her.

"Don't bug her, Alex. Felicity never comes to the beach with us. I had to bribe her," said Gwen.

"A bribe?" Alex put her arm around Felicity and said in wheedling tones, "What can I bribe you with to get you to tell me your secrets, Liss?"

"Nothing, because you're annoying." Despite her words, Felicity was still smiling, clearly used to her friends' questions.

Lucy took out the book she'd gotten at Alex's bookstore. "You have a great selection of old-school romances. I couldn't believe it when I saw this one on your shelf."

"You were in the store? I must've been on break." Alex took the book and started laughing. "I know this one! The cover is fantastic. Look at the unicorn in the corner. Why the hell is there a unicorn? It's set in New Orleans in 1885!"

"Do you ever need a reason for unicorns?" said Gwen.

"No, probably not. And look at this hunk with his rippling

pectorals." With a sly grin, Alex added, "I heard through the grapevine that you're dating Carter Roberts. That's why I wanted to meet you, you know. I might own a bookstore, but I'm actually a total slut for gossip."

"She is a slut," said Felicity, deadpan.

The three women stared at Felicity before Alex burst into laughter.

"She's right, but not like you think. I call myself a book slut." Alex elbowed Felicity. "Geez, give our new friend the wrong impression about me."

Lucy's heart warmed at the thought of being friends with these women. She hadn't had much luck making good friends in Los Angeles: the city was too big, and the acting world tended to be insular. If you weren't big—like Hayden Masterson—you were easily ignored.

"I'm not a slut, but for a guy like Carter..." Alex lay on the blanket and sighed. "You're a lucky woman, Lucy."

At the moment, Carter was playing volleyball with some of the other guys from set. Lucy had been trying—unsuccessfully—not to stare at his *ripping pectorals* as he played. It didn't help that he wore only swim trunks and nothing else. Compared to the rest of the guys, Carter was like something out of a movie: tan and muscular and so handsome that it made Lucy's heart skip a beat.

Carter might be handsome, but he's not yours. You don't want him anyway, she reminded herself.

"Do you think guys prefer virgins?" said Alex, apropos of nothing.

"Alex," Gwen admonished.

"What? It's a legitimate question."

Lucy couldn't help but notice that Felicity's right cheek—

the one without the birthmark—was red and she was pointedly not looking at Alex.

"I think they like anything that's female," joked Lucy.

Alex chuckled. "You're probably right. Besides, virgins are awkward, and you have to think about other logistics when you're getting it on."

"*Alex*," said Gwen again.

"Gwen here gets all riled whenever I bring up sex stuff." Alex sighed and sat up, stretching her legs out. "Gwen, you should read Lucy's book. Get yourself something something, if you know what I mean."

Gwen busied herself with digging around in the cooler for a soda, which Lucy had a feeling wasn't as buried as Gwen wanted them to think.

Gwen had mentioned to Lucy that she was divorced, but she hadn't volunteered any more information on that subject. When Lucy had asked if Gwen was dating anyone now, she'd clammed up and promptly told Lucy she had work to do.

Right then, Carter dove for the ball, hitting it just in time. His teammate, a crewmember whose name Lucy couldn't remember, hit the ball over the net. Carter's teammate said something and gave Carter a hand up. To Lucy's dismay, she saw Carter grimace, like he was in pain.

Should he be playing volleyball with his injured shoulder? She thought of his face when she'd come upon him pitching in the park.

"We're going to go swim. You guys want to come?" said Alex.

When Gwen declined, Lucy did so as well, mostly because she wanted to talk to Gwen alone. When her friend had asked her what she was doing, hanging out with the guy she'd claimed to hate, she'd had to dodge her questions. But Lucy was so messed up over the kiss that she had to confess it all to someone. She'd been tempted to call her older sister, Thea, but considering Thea's boyfriend was Carter's best friend and sort-of employer… Lucy had dismissed that idea quickly.

Alex jumped into the water with a squeal, while Felicity waded to where the water was about waist-high. Lucy smiled as she watched the pair.

"Good, now we can talk." Gwen turned so she faced Lucy directly. "What in the world is going on with you and Mr. Baseball? Because I heard from a little bird that you were caught making out with him in the street."

Lucy groaned, covering her face with her hands. "Oh God, I don't even know where to start."

"From the beginning, obviously."

Lucy sighed, explaining to Gwen her crush on Hayden, Carter's bargain, and how it seemed to be spinning out of control already. As Lucy spoke, Gwen's eyes kept getting bigger and bigger with each detail.

"I should call it off, right? It was a stupid idea to begin with," finished Lucy in a rush, her cheeks flaming.

Gwen didn't say anything for a long moment, lost in thought. Then she said, "Are you sure it's Hayden you're into?"

"What? Of course it's Hayden. That's why I agreed to this to begin with, and it's working. I told you that Hayden was jealous last night when he saw us together."

"But you said you'd never had a kiss like that before." Gwen sighed. "Just…be careful, okay? You're going to get hurt if you're not careful."

Lucy traced a circle in the sand. "You're saying I should tell him the deal is off."

"If I were in your shoes? Yeah, I would tell him it's off, but I'm not you. I wouldn't have agreed to something like that to begin with." Her smile was wry. "But I'm more cautious than you. Just ask Alex. She's always bugging me to be more spontaneous, to get out there and do something wild."

For some reason, Lucy hated the thought of telling Carter she was out. He'd lord it over her, anyway. He'd tell her it was because she couldn't resist him, and he'd win. The thought of him crowing and mocking her added steel to her spine. If she was excited by the thought of him kissing her again, she ignored it. That wasn't the real reason why.

Besides, they'd made progress with Hayden. Once he realized that she was truly the woman for him…

Right then, Hayden himself arrived. Instantly, the beachgoers started buzzing, taking out their phones for candid shots. Wearing only trunks, he looked like a Greek god with his golden hair and chiseled body.

But to Lucy's dismay, her heart didn't beat faster as he approached her and Gwen. Seeing him without his shirt on should make her want to throw herself at him, shouldn't it?

His gaze was heated as he took in Lucy's bikini-clad body; he barely noticed Gwen sitting next to her. "You want to play volleyball when their game is done?" he said to Lucy.

Why did she want to say no? He was the guy she wanted. Irritated with herself, she said, "Sure. But I'm not a great volleyball player, just warning you."

He shrugged. "As long as you'll say you'll play." His smile was heated as he turned away and went to the game that was still going on.

By the time Felicity and Alex returned from swimming, the second game began. On one team was Hayden and Lucy; the other was Carter and Gwen, who'd volunteered when Carter's first teammate had turned down a second game.

"We're going to cream these two," whispered Hayden. He rested his hand on her lower back; if he skimmed even an inch lower, he'd touch her bikini bottom.

Carter scowled. "Don't rough up my girlfriend," he said to Hayden.

Hayden chuckled. "I wouldn't dream of it."

Hayden served first. Lucy stood at the net, with only it between her and Carter.

"You're going down," he mouthed.

She rolled her eyes. "You wish."

Hayden's serve went high, and Carter passed the ball back over the net with ease. Despite not having played volleyball in years, Lucy's body remembered from junior high PE that she needed to hit the ball on her forearms, not her wrists. She passed the ball to Hayden, who hit it out of bounds on the other side.

Crowing, Carter picked up the ball and said, "One to zero."

"You don't get a point. It's only if you're the one serving," argued Hayden.

Lucy looked between the two men, and she half-expected them to start grappling. Gwen wrinkled her nose and mouthed to Lucy, "Men."

"We aren't playing regular volleyball. This is beach volley-ball." Carter threw the ball and caught it, not looking at Hayden, as if he weren't worth his full attention.

"We'll go with your rules," said Lucy to Carter, catching his attention finally. "If it makes you feel better."

"You're so gracious, girlfriend of mine."

Lucy flushed at his mocking words, and suddenly a spiteful little demon on her shoulder wanted to make Carter suffer. If he was going to be an asshole, she could play that game, too.

Carter served, making Hayden dive for the ball. He hit it in time for Lucy to hit it over the net. Back and forth, back and forth, until Gwen set the ball and Carter spiked it so hard that there was no way Lucy or Hayden could've caught it.

"Two to zero," said Carter.

Hayden swore under his breath before he made a show of whispering in Lucy's ear. "I'll block Carter. You stay in back."

Lucy's gaze was solely on Carter during this exchange. He seemed almost nonchalant now, but she could see the tension in his jaw. Was it all an act, to push Hayden to make his move? Or was he really jealous? That thought alone made Lucy's stomach clench.

The game continued. Soon they were neck and neck, eight to nine, with Lucy serving. Lucy served it underhand, which made it easy for Gwen to set Carter up again for a spike. This time, however, Hayden jumped and blocked Carter's spike, the ball landing out of bounds on Carter and Gwen's side.

"Awesome job!" Lucy high-fived Hayden, adrenaline pumping through her.

Hayden was sweaty and breathing hard, but he still managed to look perfectly put together. His golden hair fell across his forehead, and his smile was radiant as he looked down at Lucy.

"One more point and we tie the game. We got this," he said.

He touched her shoulder in a caress that made her shiver. But to her surprise, she found herself stepping back and saying, "I need to serve."

Her mind was whirling as they played the next round. Didn't she want Hayden to touch her? She wished she could understand herself, but it was like she was her own enigma.

"Set me!" said Hayden as he hit the ball to Lucy.

Lucy set the ball to allow Hayden to spike it over the net. Carter dove for the spiked ball, landing on his right side. Even though he hit the ball, it careened into the net and fell to the sand before Gwen could reach it.

Hayden yelled in triumph and picked up Lucy, whirling her around. She laughed in surprise, but when Hayden set her down and she looked over at Carter, the laughter died in her throat.

Carter's face was pale as he rose from the sand. "Are you okay?" Gwen asked him in a low voice.

He shook his head, but he didn't let Gwen help him up. Of course he wouldn't: he was too proud to ask for help, thought Lucy sadly.

"Good game," said Carter, extending his hand to Hayden.

Hayden smirked and finally shook Carter's hand. "Until next time."

Carter stalked off; Lucy almost went after him, when Hayden said to her, "You were pretty impressive, you know."

"I wasn't that great. You were the one who spiked that last ball."

"But you set me up for it. We make a good team, don't we?" His smile was like a caress across her skin, and she was reminded again of how long she'd been crushing on this man. How she'd dreamed of a moment like this.

But when she saw Carter out of the corner of her eye, she said quickly, "I need to go get something out of my car. I'll be right back."

She didn't know why she was following Carter when Hayden was right there, hers for the plucking. She knew that, but as she came around the side of Carter's SUV and saw him sitting in the open hatchback, she didn't care about anything that had to do with Hayden Masterson right then.

"I knew it. You landed on your shoulder, didn't you?" said Lucy.

"I'm fine. Go back to your golden boy." He winced as he reached for his t-shirt, his face going even paler.

"You're not fine. You look like you're going to puke." Lucy, not caring if she got bit in the process, touched his forehead.

"I don't have a fever, Mom," said Carter wryly, but he didn't push her away.

Lucy couldn't stop herself from touching his cheek, feeling the bristle of his beard against her palm. "You should probably go to the ER. What if you reinjured it?"

"I'm not going to some tiny ER to wait three hours. I need to get back and ice it."

"Then I'll drive you back."

"No." Carter softened his tone at her expression. "No, it's fine. Go back to the beach."

Lucy hadn't yet moved away from him, and she had no interest in doing so. She didn't know what it was about this man, why he was the one who'd captivated her from the first moment. He was all hard angles and sharp edges, and he had walls that wrapped around him like a fortress. Yet Lucy couldn't stay away from him.

"Lucy," said Hayden behind her.

Lucy froze; Carter's warm gaze turned icy.

"Are you coming back? We're having drinks to celebrate," said Hayden.

Lucy stared into Carter's eyes, as if she were waiting for him to give her permission. She should be elated that Hayden had come to find her. *I should feel this, I should feel that. So many shoulds that I seem incapable of doing.*

"Your lover boy is waiting for you," said Carter acidly. "You don't need to keep doing this show for him."

Lucy jerked away, hurt spreading through her. "Do you think I came up here just for show? Carter—"

Carter waved a hand and stood up. "You got what you wanted, little spitfire," he murmured in her ear. "Go get him."

"Lucy?" said Hayden a second time. "Are you coming?"

"I'll be right there. I need to talk to Carter."

Finally, Hayden left, and Lucy followed Carter to the driver's side of the car.

"What the hell was that all about?" she hissed. "Do you really think I didn't care if you'd hurt yourself?"

"I never said that. You have basic human decency, but don't tell me you did it solely out of concern for me. If it meant furthering your goal to get Hayden, then why not?" Carter shrugged, then grimaced.

"It wasn't...I didn't." Lucy shook her head, mostly because she didn't know why she'd come up here. Was Carter right, that she'd done it for selfish reasons? She felt sick to her stomach.

"Look, I don't care what your reasons were. Our deal was to make your lover boy jealous, and that's what we're doing."

"Yeah, I guess," said Lucy hollowly. She wrapped her arms

around herself, suddenly cold. "Then we don't need to keep doing this, do we?"

Carter's expression grew shuttered. "I guess we don't. You won, little spitfire. Hayden is yours for the taking."

After Carter had driven off, Lucy knew she should be elated. She'd captured the attention of Hayden Masterson, the man that every woman in the world wanted.

So why did she feel like she'd lost something irreplaceable instead?

CHAPTER TEN

Another week passed in the blink of an eye. Lucy's days and sometimes nights were kept busy with filming.

On her fourth evening working overtime, Lucy was in rehearsals with Hayden once again. They'd gotten into a routine together: warming up in the morning and going over lines, rehearsal if necessary, then onto filming.

Hayden, though, proved to be a total perfectionist. He would often demand multiple takes, sometimes for his own performances, but other times for other actors'. One afternoon they did twenty takes for a ten-second scene. Jim, despite his best efforts, didn't have enough sway to ignore what their star actor wanted.

Lucy was glad that Hayden's wrath didn't land on her very often, and if it did, it was tempered with a flirtatious smile. Lucy knew that Hayden was into her: he touched her whenever he got a chance, and he flirted with her so blatantly that Erin had commented on it.

Now, Lucy was in Hayden's trailer working on the

upcoming scene that was going to be filmed that day. After multiple rounds, Hayden said, "I think we got it, as long as you say that line with tons of emotion. The fifth time was the best one."

Lucy made a note on her script. Sometimes she wished that Hayden wasn't such a micromanager of everyone around him, but she didn't have the guts to tell him to back off. Besides, he was the Oscar-nominated actor, not her. She was lucky to receive so much direction from him.

"Can you make some coffee? Linda always brings me some, but she's sick today." Hayden rolled his eyes. "She's always getting sick. I'm tempted to find a new assistant altogether."

Lucy didn't comment on the fact that she'd seen Linda this morning looking very green. She doubted Linda wanted to be sick. She also didn't feel like telling Hayden to make coffee himself, although she couldn't help but feel irritation build inside her at his demand.

"So, what's happening between you and Carter?" said Hayden. He sat down on his couch, putting his legs up on the coffee table. His trailer was the biggest one on the lot, with a mini-kitchen, living room, and bedroom, even though he was staying in his own cottage on the island. Empty bottles of imported water and kombucha were scattered throughout the trailer. Lucy was pretty sure that Hayden ate nothing but salmon, açai berries, and air. When Lucy had eaten a donut in front of him once, he'd grimaced like she'd infect him with donut germs.

Hearing Carter's name, Lucy froze, her heart in her throat. She hadn't seen Carter all week, even though they were staying at the same bed-and-breakfast. Did Hayden know that they were no longer together? But they hadn't been really *together* in the first place, either.

"I think the pot is filled," said Hayden.

Lucy looked down to see water overflowing the coffeepot. Blushing, she shut the water off, dumped the excess water, and finally managed to start the coffee brewing. She sat down across from Hayden, her palms sweaty.

"So?" Hayden cocked an eyebrow. "Are you guys official now?"

"What would make us official?"

"You tell me."

"Well, it's not like we've changed our statuses on Facebook to 'in a relationship,' if that's what you're asking."

Hayden considered her, then sighed. "I didn't want to do this, but I thought I should warn you about Carter Roberts. We're in similar circles. I mean, he's not an actor, of course, but he's as famous as I am. He gets his fair share of tabloid stories and gossip columns."

"That's not exactly a secret, you know."

"I'm getting to it. Carter, well, he's not the kind of guy who sticks around." Hayden shrugged. "We actually dated the same woman." Seeing Lucy's expression, he said with a laugh, "Not at the same time. I'm not that kinky." He winked.

Lucy laughed, but it sounded hollow to her ears.

"Rosie—she's my ex, you know. She dated Carter for a few months. She thought he was the real deal, that he was going to commit. Talked about marriage, all that shit. Then she comes home one day to find him fucking another woman. She was really torn up about it."

Lucy felt her blood chill in her veins. She'd known Carter was a playboy, but she hadn't pegged him as a cheater.

"The worst thing wasn't even the cheating," continued Hayden, "but the fact that he'd played all these mind games with her. Telling her one thing, doing another. It was messed up. And he kept blowing up her phone. Texting her all hours of the night. She almost got a restraining order. He was like some crazy stalker."

Lucy heard the coffeepot beep, but the smell of coffee suddenly made her nauseous. "Why are you telling me this?"

"Be careful. Carter comes off like one thing when he's actually another. And you haven't been in this industry long enough to know when somebody is playing you," he said, his tone gentle.

"Don't worry," she said, her mind in turmoil. "I won't do anything stupid."

"I'm sure you won't." Hayden glanced over at the coffeepot. "Can you get me a mug? I'm feeling too lazy to get up."

After she'd poured them both a cup of coffee, Lucy sat in silence as she looked at her phone. But she wasn't actually reading anything: her mind was whirling with what Hayden had told her. Had she been naive to get involved with him? But he'd already told her that their deal was over. She'd gotten Hayden's attention. She could tell Hayden right now that she and Carter were done for, that she liked *him*, that she'd made a mistake in dating Carter.

She could, but she didn't. It was like the words she knew she needed to say were impossible to speak. Besides, she didn't want to admit to Hayden that she'd made a mistake and that he'd been right about Carter.

She felt sick to her stomach all morning, even when Lucy made some vague excuse and went to her own trailer for some privacy. The memories of how naive she'd been pushed to the forefront of her brain.

A year ago, before she'd ever met Hayden, Lucy had won the lead part in a play at a well-respected small theater in Los Angeles. She'd been thrilled, because a number of now-famous actors had done gigs at this very theater early in their careers. She'd expected to form connections that could boost her career.

The theater owner was a middle-aged man who knew everyone you needed to know in Hollywood. Glen took Lucy under his wing at the very beginning. Lucy considered it a compliment, grateful that she'd caught the eye of someone who was a bastion in the acting community.

But one night after everyone else left, Lucy stayed behind to talk to Glen about one scene. He told her to come to his office.

Lucy pulled out her script, pointing to one of the lines. "This one keeps tripping me up. I know you said it should be filled with pathos, but it doesn't seem like something Tracy would say."

Glen came around the other side of the desk, leaning over Lucy. To her surprise, he put his hand on her shoulder.

"But isn't Tracy wanting to get Felix's attention? Isn't it more about her desires than anything else?" said Glen.

Lucy waited for him to move his hand from her shoulder, but he only squeezed it. *He's just overly friendly*, she told herself. *He doesn't mean anything by it.*

"I mean, she does," said Lucy hesitantly, "but I guess this line makes her sound more bitter than I think she is."

"Hmm, I never thought about it like that." Glen leaned down until his cheek was almost pressing against Lucy's. "Which line precisely are you talking about?"

Lucy pointed, and Glen reached around her, brushing against the side of her breast as he did so. When he cupped her breast for a long moment, she couldn't breathe. *This isn't happening*, she kept telling herself. *It was an accident. He's older. He doesn't know what he's doing.*

"Oh, I see what you mean. I'll edit that line," said Glen companionably. He finally stood, but not before he caressed Lucy's shoulder one last time.

For the rest of the production, Lucy avoided being alone with Glen as much as possible. She never stayed late; she never arrived early. If she happened to be in the dressing room alone, she always locked the door. More than once, her castmates had to knock on the door and ask why it had been locked, Lucy acting like she hadn't realized that it had been locked all along.

She thought about reporting Glen, but she told herself she'd overreacted. He hadn't hurt her, and he hadn't threatened her. He'd been too handsy. She made up all kinds of excuses for him, mostly because it was easier to push it under the rug than confront the fact that her director had sexually harassed her.

The last performance ended with Glen cornering Lucy in the dressing room. She thought she'd locked the door since she was alone, but maybe she'd forgotten in the excitement of the play ending. Her heart in her throat, she tried to leave, but Glen was persistent. He was bigger than her, and he was her boss. If she did anything he didn't like, he could blackball her in the entire community if he wanted to.

"Why are you so tense?" He once again began to rub her shoulders. "Your performance tonight was amazing, you know."

"Thank you." She felt his hands move down her back. When he pushed the strap of her tank off her shoulder, she jumped up, stuttering, "I need to go to the bathroom."

"Lucy, don't be like that. I've seen how you look at me. Don't deny it. I can show you a good time, if you'll let me."

When she looked back on this, she wished she'd been brave like her sister Thea. Thea would've kneed Glen in the balls and called him a gross motherfucker. Lucy, though, had never been as ballsy—literally and figuratively—as her older sister. She tended to believe that most people were decent and fair, and whenever she ran into someone who wasn't, she couldn't understand why.

Maybe that made her naive, or just stupid. She didn't know anymore.

"Thank you, but no," she said, hoping Glen didn't react badly to her turning him down.

"Why are you playing hard to get?" He moved until she was pressed up against one of the dressing tables. "Don't be a tease, Lucy. We both know you'll give in."

It was only Lucy's castmate Gretchen coming into the dressing room that kept the situation from turning into something worse. Glen stood up, muttered some excuse, and left the room before either Lucy or Gretchen could say anything. But Gretchen, older than Lucy and hardened by this work, saw the look on her face and had demanded to know what had happened.

Lucy had struggled to find work after that. Glen had blackballed her as much as he could, taking her rejection as a slight against him. Depressed and anxious, Lucy had almost given up acting entirely because everything had seemed so pointless. It was only her agent getting her the gig for *The Last Goodbye* that had stopped her from packing up her things and returning home to Fair Haven, Washington.

Her thoughts turned to Hayden's accusations toward Carter. Had he really harassed his ex-girlfriend and cheated on her? But why would Hayden lie about something like that? Her stomach turned thinking about it.

The only good thing was that she and Carter had called off this deal between them. But for whatever reason, she didn't find that thought as comforting as she should. More than that, she wanted a reason to believe that Carter was innocent. That the man who she couldn't stop thinking about was decent and good, even if he was obnoxious and arrogant and sexy and guarded and he had dimples when he smiled—

A knock on Lucy's trailer door made her jump. "Lucy," said Erin through the door, "we need to get to set!"

Lucy pushed her whirling thoughts aside. At least she knew how to act like nothing was bothering her.

"I DON'T KNOW what you want from me!" cried Lucy-as-Miranda. She threw her hands up in defeat. "You tell me one thing and do another. Why can't you leave me alone?"

Hayden-as-Malcolm stalked toward Miranda, growling low in his throat. "Why do you think? Because I'm fucking in love with you, that's why!"

Carter stood on set and watched the scene, arms crossed.

He didn't normally watch filming, but when he'd heard that the penultimate scene was filming today, his curiosity had gotten the better of him. Besides, he liked watching Lucy work. She transformed completely, and when she acted, he almost forgot she was his little spitfire instead of Miranda.

She's not your anything, he reminded himself. Yes, she'd made that more than clear that day at the beach. Besides, she'd gotten what she wanted. Carter had lost the bet—or deal, whatever you wanted to call it—and Lucy had won. That was how the cookie had crumbled.

Okay, maybe he wasn't so resigned to the idea of Lucy and Hayden together. He'd loved imagining Hayden pissing himself when Carter stole the woman he wanted, like Hayden had done to Carter. It was petty, but sometimes all a guy had was pettiness and spite to fuel him through the day.

Hayden-as-Malcolm embraced Lucy-as-Miranda and kissed her, open-mouthed and deep. Miranda clung to Hayden's shoulder like her knees were wobbly, and Carter couldn't help but wonder if she was just acting or was really as into the kiss as she seemed.

Why was he doing this to himself? He obviously needed to get laid. He'd go to some bar tonight and find a willing woman or two. If he could get rid of this obsession with Lucy, he wouldn't give two shits who she decided to screw.

During a break, Carter was talking to Pamela when Hayden joined the conversation. Soon, it was just Hayden and Carter, and Carter wasn't about to be the first one to scamper away.

Lucy was talking with one of her castmates, her smile wide as she laughed. Carter's stomach clenched.

"She's something, isn't she?" remarked Hayden. "She's been great to work with."

"Congratulations," said Carter, sarcasm dripping from his voice.

"She's still new enough that she hasn't let this industry make her bitter. I've met too many actresses who have aged ten years in six months from the bullshit they put us through." Hayden chuckled, although Carter didn't know what was funny about that remark. "Lucy, though—she's fresh. Innocent. It's alluring."

Carter snorted. "This sounds like shit you should write in your diary."

"I want her," said Hayden. "Is she yours or not?"

Carter stared at Hayden. What the hell kind of game was he playing? "Since when do you ask for permission?" Because Hayden hadn't cared that Rosie was Carter's girlfriend when he'd swooped in and stolen her from him.

"This time I'm asking: what's Lucy to you?"

Carter watched Lucy's hands move as she talked. He'd always heard some people described as "lighting up the room," but Lucy didn't just light it up: she illuminated every nook and cranny. She was light bottled in a woman's body. He'd never met anyone like her.

And if she wanted Hayden Masterson, Carter wasn't going to stand in the way any longer. Besides, he should let her go. She'd hate him if she ever found out he'd made this bargain with her only to fuck with Hayden.

"Us? There is no us," said Carter finally. "We weren't doing anything but having a good time, if that's what you want to know."

Hayden grinned. "Excellent." He slapped Carter on the back like they were old pals. "Thanks, man."

Carter didn't stay to watch the rest of the filming. He drove straight to Murphy's, the one dive bar on the entire island, and started working on getting totally hammered.

CHAPTER ELEVEN

Carter picked up his glass, only to realize that it was already empty. How many drinks had he had? He'd lost count. To his immense irritation, he was only vaguely buzzed. It was just his luck that he couldn't get drunk off his ass like he wanted to.

He was considering whether or not he wanted to go back to his room and sleep or get another beer when a woman sat down next to him at the bar, wearing a skimpy top and even shorter skirt. The woman's breasts were close to spilling from her top if she moved too quickly. She smiled flirtatiously at Carter, her lips bright pink and pouting.

"You're that ballplayer, aren't you?" she said, a slight drawl to her words. "Basketball, right?"

Carter couldn't help but stare at her breasts: he was human and male, after all. She certainly had enough of them to get the attention of any straight male in this greasy little dive bar.

"Close," said Carter. "Baseball."

"Oh, even better. The way you guys handle those balls…" She fluttered her eyelashes.

Carter almost choked. He waved at the bartender and said in a croaking voice, "Another beer. And something for my friend here."

"Whiskey sour." The woman turned on the stool until she faced Carter. "I'm Kelly, by the way."

"Carter."

Her eyes widened. "Oh, I know who you are now. I'd heard you were in town, but I didn't believe it. What's a big star pitcher like you doing in tiny ole Hazel Island? Are you on vacation?"

"Worse: I'm working."

"On baseball?"

He chuckled darkly. "No, I'm benched. You didn't hear that part, darlin'? No, I'm working on this movie that's been filming."

"I got Hayden Masterson's autograph the other day." Kelly sighed happily. "That man could seduce a nun if he wanted to."

The reminder of Hayden's seduction skills soured Carter's mood further. Normally he'd at least be interested in any woman throwing herself at him, but tonight he felt like he was pulling out his own teeth to give a shit. And that annoyed him further, because he knew the reason why he was so distracted.

His little spitfire wasn't going to ruin his evening more than she already had. Forcing her out of his mind, he gave Kelly his most winning smile.

"Did you come sit by me just to talk about another man?" He cocked an eyebrow.

Kelly giggled. "No, of course not. Hayden has nothing on

you." She took in his appearance, licking her lips. "He's not near so…big as you."

She wasn't subtle, that was for sure, but Carter didn't have time for subtlety. He wasn't going to turn an attractive woman away because she was giving off signals like a lighthouse in a storm.

"I'm surprised he let you get away from him." Carter's gaze went to her cleavage and then slowly traveled back to her face. "I wouldn't have, you know."

"I know you wouldn't have. That's why I'm sitting here right now." She brushed her foot against his leg and sipped her whiskey sour in obvious invitation.

Carter's body responded to Kelly's cues, but halfheartedly, as if it felt compelled to respond against its better judgment. Carter wondered if he'd simply drunk too much tonight. Pushing his beer away, he asked for a glass of water and some fries to share with Kelly. Maybe if he sobered up a bit, he'd get back to how he usually was.

But as he and Kelly chatted and flirted, munching on French fries, Carter's interest in her only waned. It kept decreasing with every giggle, every hair flip, and every brush of her foot against his leg. When she leaned over his arm to reach the last of the fries, her breasts on full display, the only thing he felt was bored.

Bored. Breasts bored him now. He needed to get his shit together already.

"You ready to go?" said Carter abruptly after he paid his tab.

Kelly raised her eyebrows but just smiled. "Sure. You staying close by? Otherwise we could go to my place. It's only a few miles from here."

The last thing he needed was to run into Lucy. "Let's go to your place."

Carter was sober enough now that he offered to drive. When he was about to open the passenger door for Kelly, she wrapped herself around him and kissed him.

Carter's body stirred—finally. He deepened the kiss, running his hands down her torso, her breasts crushed against his chest. She made little mewling sounds in her throat. It sounded like a kitten drowning, if he was honest.

That stirring? It deflated. Completely. It didn't help that Kelly kept wiggling and moaning, like she was about to orgasm right there in the street.

Then he had the worst thought of all: *I can't do this.*

"You know what?" he said. "Not tonight."

"I can drive, if you're worried about that," she purred.

"Not tonight." He was firmer now, gently pushing her hands away from his belt buckle. "I'll walk you to your car."

Hurt crossed her face, but she masked it quickly. Then she shrugged. "I can walk myself. Enjoy your night."

Carter knew very well that he wasn't going to enjoy anything tonight. He was confused, tired, and pissed off. And he wished he hadn't sobered up because right then he wanted to be rip-roaring drunk.

He stopped at a liquor store and bought a nice bottle of scotch. Once he arrived back at the bed-and-breakfast, he didn't even change his clothes before he popped the bottle open.

Lucy. Lucy Lucy Lucy, his mind kept repeating. He saw her eyes when he'd kissed her; he felt how she'd responded to his touch. He saw how she'd kissed Hayden today while filming, knowing that she'd been acting but not remotely convinced she had been.

How had one little spitfire ruined him for other women? Aching at the thought of kissing her again, his cock hard when it hadn't been with Kelly, he drank through the night in the hopes that he could extinguish whatever this was inside of him.

WHEN LUCY STEPPED into the entrance of the bed-and-breakfast, she was breathless and flushed. She looked around, hoping she could slip up to her room without anyone noticing her.

No such luck.

Gwen stepped out from the meeting room, took one look at Lucy, and said, "What did you do?"

"Nothing!" Even to Lucy's ears, her voice was shrill.

Gwen pointed to the kitchen. "Get in there and tell me what's up before I beat it out of you."

Lucy didn't put up much of a protest, mostly because she knew that she'd get some cookies leftover from this morning to munch on. While Gwen put a kettle on to boil—the kitchen about one and a half times the size of a normal kitchen— Lucy fiddled with the hair tie she'd put on her wrist.

Gwen set two cups of tea down and a plate of peanut butter cookies, Lucy's favorite. As Lucy reached for one, though, Gwen pulled the plate back.

"Spill, woman. I don't make tea for free."

"God, you're mean." Lucy grabbed a cookie and then blurted, "Hayden asked me out."

Gwen stilled, her eyebrows practically near her hairline. Lucy hadn't told her about her conversation with Carter after he'd hurt his shoulder at the beach, mostly because Lucy hadn't yet figured out how she felt about it.

After filming today, Hayden had been so charming, so flirtatious, that when he'd asked her to go out to dinner on Saturday, Lucy hadn't been able to find an excuse to say no. And why should she? Hayden Masterson had asked her *out*. It was every girl's dream come true. It was her dream come true, yet she was still waiting to feel that sense of elation.

"You don't sound very excited about it," said Gwen as she bit into a cookie. "Did you say yes?"

Lucy nodded. "Who would say no to a date with a guy like Hayden?"

"Well, somebody who was into another guy might."

Her heart pounding like crazy, Lucy hoped that Gwen couldn't see how red her cheeks had gotten in the dim light. "I've had a crush on Hayden for a year."

"So? Feelings change. And you met him, what, once? You didn't know him. You wanted to get to know him, but that's not the same thing."

It sounded so simple when Gwen said it, but it wasn't that simple. Lucy had felt a connection with Hayden, and obviously he felt the same thing since he'd asked her out.

"Look, I'm the last person who anyone should go to for advice on romance," said Gwen wryly. "I'm a divorcee and I hate dating. I haven't been on a date in almost a year at this point. That being said, don't deny what you're feeling because you think your feelings should fit into one box and they don't."

Lucy stared at the steam rising from her tea. She felt like a jigsaw puzzle that had become a jumbled mess of random pieces. She closed her eyes and forced herself to take a deep breath.

"I don't know what I want," she finally said truthfully.

"That's okay. We've all been there. But if you can't be honest with yourself, you can't be honest with a partner." Gwen gazed off into the distance, like she was remembering something. Her gaze grew shuttered.

"Is that what happened to you? Why you got divorced?" Lucy knew she was treading on a sensitive subject, but she couldn't help her curiosity. She and Gwen had gotten close these past few weeks, but Gwen had yet to volunteer even this much information about her marriage.

Gwen's mouth twisted. "You could say it was. Or really, I wasn't what he wanted me to be." She fell silent and pensive.

Lucy, not wanting to be alone, changed the subject, and soon she and Gwen were chatting into the night. They finished off the cookies, had another cup of tea each, and finally called it a night when they both couldn't stop yawning.

Lucy headed upstairs to her room. The bed-and-breakfast was still, most everyone asleep in their beds. The place managed to feel both homey and up-to-date, with local artists' works on the walls and the paint a cheerful buttercup. The place housed up to fifteen people at a time. Since there were more than fifteen people working on *The Last Goodbye*, the crew had to find lodging elsewhere or simply ride the ferry every day from the town across the water.

A door opened down the hallway. To Lucy's consternation, it was Carter, the last person she wanted to see.

She tried to get inside her room before he stopped her, but she wasn't fast enough. She still unlocked her door, but Carter stuck his foot in the doorway, stopping her from getting inside.

"Do you need something?" she said. She wrinkled her nose when she smelled the alcohol on his breath. "Are you drunk?"

Carter snorted. "I wish. More like happily buzzed." He peered down at her. "Where were you tonight?"

He was definitely drunker than he'd copped to. Rolling her eyes, she pushed at his arm. "None of your business. I'm going to bed. You should, too."

"No, tell me. Were you with him?"

Lucy's heart seized in her chest. As she looked up at Carter, his smile lazy yet dangerously feral, irritation made her strike back at this man who'd plagued her for weeks.

"He asked me out for dinner. There, are you happy? Is that what you wanted to hear?" she said in triumph.

Carter kept smiling. "You got what you wanted, little spitfire. Congratulations. I hope he remembers to wear a rubber when you fuck. Otherwise, you might catch something. He's stuck his dick in plenty of women already."

Lucy's face flamed with humiliation and disgust. "What the hell is your problem? Are you really going to play dog in the manger? Besides, like you're one to talk. Didn't you tell me your number one hobby was fucking?"

Leaning down, he whispered in her ear, "Yes, and I'm sure you imagined me doing it to you. How I'd touch you, make you come with my fingers. Then my mouth, but I wouldn't make it easy. I'd make you beg until you could only say my name."

His words washed over her, flames igniting deep in her belly. Trembling, she whispered, "You're wrong."

"No, I'm not." He sounded almost sad. "You're not that good of an actress, babe."

Lucy scowled. Throwing her arm around his neck, she brought his head down and kissed him—hard. She pushed her tongue into his mouth like an invader to prove to herself that she didn't want him. Not really. He disgusted her, enraged her. He made her want the complete opposite of him.

It took a millisecond for Carter to overcome his shock. Then he had his fingers tangled in her hair. He held her until their bodies aligned, and she felt his hardness against her belly. Shivering uncontrollably, she felt tears prick her eyes when he started to kiss her throat.

She opened her eyes, and for the first time, she saw that he had a pink lip-print on his neck. Had he slept with another woman tonight? And then he'd come to her room afterward?

Her blood turned to ice; she felt sick to her stomach.

"No, no." Her voice wasn't working. She shook her head and said more loudly, "Don't touch me. Don't touch me!"

Carter froze. Then he stepped away from her.

They were both breathing hard. Lucy could see the outline of his erection against his jeans, and it took all of her willpower not to throw herself into his arms again. Whatever this was between them—it could only end badly. Carter wasn't the type of man she'd dreamed of falling in love with. This, this thing? It was just lust, and after Carter had had his fill of her, he'd go on his merry way.

Lucy refused to be another notch on his bedpost. He could sleep with whomever he wanted; she wasn't going to be one of them. She remembered Hayden warning her about Carter. This was confirmation that what Hayden had said must be true.

"I'm going on a date with Hayden," she whispered.

Carter said nothing.

"I'm going on a date with him, and I want you to leave me alone." She swallowed. "Please."

Something crossed his face that she didn't recognize. If she were crazy, she'd almost think he was hurt. But then he shrugged and said softly, "Good night."

And then she was alone.

CHAPTER TWELVE

Soft jazz flowed around Lucy as she gazed out onto the sunset over the water. It was gorgeous, the spill of colors fanning across the sky. Sipping her wine, she felt a sense of calm fill her for the first time in three days.

"Did I tell you how beautiful you look tonight?" said Hayden. He raised his own wineglass in a toast.

"I think you said it at least twice, but it's nice to hear again anyway."

Tonight she wore one of her favorite dresses: a short little black dress with slim straps that set off the milkiness of her skin. She wore pearl earrings, her hair in a loose braid around her head. She felt a bit like Audrey Hepburn; all she needed was a cigarette and a guitar and she'd play a perfect Holly Golightly.

Hayden had taken Lucy to one of the nicest restaurants on Hazel Island: situated on the tip of the northern part of the island, it overlooked the water. Since it was summer, most of the restaurant-goers sat outside, tall heaters keeping the patio warm as the sun set and the temperature dropped.

Lucy had ordered oysters on the half shell, her absolute favorite. She was almost as excited for the food as she was to be on a date with Hayden Masterson.

She knew she was getting stares as she sat with him. She knew that even in a place like Hazel Island, there were people with phones taking photos and posting them online. By tomorrow morning, there would be articles about Hayden's mysterious new lady.

A knot of anxiety had formed in Lucy's stomach, thinking of being talked about in gossip columns and blogs. She should be used to being talked about, but she'd never had her personal life discussed. She hoped nobody dug too deep into her past. She didn't have anything to hide exactly, but some things she'd rather not have strangers commenting over, like they actually knew her.

"How's the pinot noir?" said the waiter.

Hayden swirled his wine and shrugged. "I've had better. Do you want another bottle of this one, Lucy?"

Lucy didn't know why she'd order a wine neither of them really liked. "This is fine," she said.

"She means she wants a white wine. Women always prefer white," said Hayden. Once the waiter left, he said to Lucy, "I wasn't sure how this place would be. Despite the great reviews, I'm not impressed."

"Just because you didn't like the wine?"

"I guess you wouldn't know what was really five-star or not." His smile was edged with condescension.

Lucy bit back a sharp retort. If this was Hayden's way of wooing her, he was doing a terrible job at it. At least Carter had never treated her like she was stupid.

Her heart flip-flopped in her chest. After that kiss, Lucy

had been so out of sorts that she'd considered calling in sick for filming. The thought of running into Carter on set would've been too much to bear. But Erin had dragged her out of bed, and luckily for Lucy, Carter hadn't been on set that day. She hadn't seen him since that night.

When their food arrived, Lucy was glad for the distraction. Hayden seemed content to talk trash about the restaurant, all the while drinking the wine he supposedly didn't like. Lucy almost moaned when she ate her first oyster: whatever Hayden thought, this place had divine oysters. She'd eat an entire bucket of them if she could.

Hayden carved into his filet mignon and frowned. "Why can no one cook a steak medium rare?" He waved the waiter down with an impatient gesture. "Send this back. It's still raw."

A few minutes later, the waiter returned with Hayden's plate and a newly cooked filet. To Lucy's surprise, he sent the second back one, too. It was only on the third try that Hayden grudgingly ate his food, muttering about shitty restaurants the entire time.

Had Hayden always been this…annoying? Lucy didn't know if he was having an off day or if he was always like this.

When Hayden paid the check and went to use the men's room, Lucy couldn't help herself. She peeked at the receipt to see that Hayden had written on the line for the tip: $0. Horrified, Lucy dug around in her purse for some cash and stuffed it into the leather holder before Hayden returned.

Hayden had invited Lucy out to his cottage that evening, but at the moment, she was tempted to call it a night. As Hayden opened the passenger door for her, he took one look at her face and said, "What's wrong?"

Lucy pulled her coat closer. She considered lying, but she couldn't help herself. "Why didn't you tip the waiter? He didn't do anything wrong."

Hayden's eyes widened. Then he chuckled. "Is that what you're worried about? Darling, these places include gratuity in the bill. You can add a tip on top, if you like, but I didn't think I needed to."

Lucy hadn't heard of any places in America doing such a thing, even though it made more sense than their current system. But not wanting to push her luck, she said, "Sorry. My mistake."

"You're cute when you're riled." Hayden touched her arm. "Let's go to my place. I have real wine there, too."

Lucy had to admit, Hayden's cottage was hardly a cottage in the traditional sense of the word. It was more like a mini-mansion, with two floors, a long, winding driveway, and even a fountain out front.

"Nobody actually lives here full-time?" she said to Hayden. "I'm surprised no one is using this place during the summer, at least."

Hayden shrugged. "No idea. The studio booked it for me. The owner probably has other properties he can stay in. Besides, this place isn't all that big. But I guess you can't expect anything more on this tiny island."

The interior of the "cottage" was all modern, the floors a glossy pine, the walls covered with modern art. A piano sat in the corner of the open living room. What she assumed were Hayden's things—bottles and food containers—were scattered across the kitchen table.

When Hayden saw what she was looking at, he shook his

head. "Crazy, right? There's no housekeeping service out here. They'll have to clean up after I leave, I guess."

Lucy hadn't been thinking that in the slightest, but she didn't feel like saying as much. When Hayden offered her a glass of white wine, she was glad to drink something. Maybe a little more alcohol would improve her mood.

Hayden turned on music and dimmed the lights. Lucy gazed out onto the water: now that it was dark, she could only see the moon's reflection on it. She wished she had a boat: she could row to the middle of the sea, the only sounds the lapping of waves and her own heartbeat.

"What are you thinking about?" said Hayden.

"Nothing. Everything." She smiled, turning her head. "Why did you want to become an actor?" she said suddenly.

"Because I was good at it. Better at it than sports, I'll say that."

At the mention of sports, Lucy's thoughts darted straight to Carter. Her hand tightened around the stem of her wineglass. Was he looking out at the moon right now, wondering about her? *Of course he's not. He's probably found another woman to screw in your absence.*

"But when did you know it was what you wanted to do?" she insisted. "Was there some moment or performance as a kid where you thought, 'This is it'?"

Hayden considered her. "Not that I can think of. I didn't really do much acting as a kid. I did some theater in high school, but that was it. Then I got picked up by an agent who saw me in an off-Broadway play my senior year, and that was it. Now here I am."

"No living in a cockroach-infested apartment with five other roommates for you, huh?"

Hayden set down his wineglass on the piano before taking Lucy's glass from her as well. "Does it matter?" he said. He wrapped one arm around her waist, bringing her closer.

Her heart in her throat, Lucy waited for Hayden's next move. Would he try to kiss her? She wished he would, she thought, because then maybe she could get Carter out of her head once and for all.

Hayden tilted her chin up, his touch gentle. Lucy closed her eyes. As he pressed his mouth to hers, she held her breath.

The kiss was good—great, even. Hayden knew how to seduce a woman with just his lips. He was confident but searching, neither completely taking nor receiving. Lucy tangled her hands in his hair, and he let out a grunt.

She waited for the fireworks. She waited for that feeling of the world fading away around her. She waited—and it never came.

She could hear an airplane flying; she smelled wine and sandalwood, and it made her head hurt. And when she opened her eyes while still kissing Hayden, she knew.

She knew that she'd been the biggest idiot in the history of the universe. Her crush on Hayden had been merely a fantasy. The real thing, though, didn't affect her like she'd thought it would.

He didn't make her heart race like Carter Roberts did.

Lucy ended the kiss, trying to step away. She needed to tell Hayden…something. Some ridiculous excuse that wouldn't sour their working relationship too much.

"I can't," she said, because that was all she could think of right now.

"You can't what?"

"I don't think this is a good idea. Since we're working together and all."

Hayden's smile was placating. "You really are just a baby, aren't you? Actors have been hooking up with each other on movie sets since the dawn of filmmaking. Nobody cares, Lucy."

"I know that." Irritation bubbled up inside her. She put more space between them. "It's not that it's wrong, necessarily. Just not wise."

"If you thought it was a bad idea, then why did you agree to go out with me? And to come here?" Annoyance laced his tone. He picked up his forgotten wineglass and drained it in one gulp.

He had a point. Lucy's shoulders slumped. "I'm sorry. Can you take me back to the bed-and-breakfast?"

He picked up her glass of wine and drained that one, too, then said in a faux-apologetic voice, "Sorry, babe. Can't drive right now. You can either wait or call a cab to come get you." He touched her arm as he once again embraced her. "Or you could enjoy yourself and stop thinking so much."

When he kissed her this time, Lucy struggled and pushed hard at his chest. "Stop—stop!"

He did, to her immense relief. But his gaze was scathing as he took in her flushed appearance. "Suit yourself." Then he stalked away, more than likely to find the open wine bottle.

Tears pressed against Lucy's eyelids. Embarrassed and horrified, she grabbed her coat and purse and decided that she'd rather walk than wait for Hayden to sober up. She could ask to use his car, but then she'd have to bring it back to him. No way in hell was she coming back to this place.

As she began walking, though, she realized how far it was

to downtown. It was probably three miles, which would've been easy for Lucy if she weren't wearing heels and walking alone in the dark. When she tried to pull up the Internet on her phone, she realized she had no service out here, and she didn't exactly have a number for a cab company. Did Hazel Island even have taxis?

She tried to call Gwen, but the call kept dropping before Gwen even picked up. Lucy let out a screech of rage. Not knowing what else to do, she kept walking, hoping she didn't twist an ankle in the dark.

She'd walked about a half mile when her feet ached so badly that she needed to sit down. As she rounded the corner of the deserted sidewalk that she hoped led in the right direction, the distant sound of the sea came closer. She kept walking in that direction, and soon she reached a tiny beach.

No one was on the beach, of course, but at least there was more light from a few flickering streetlamps. Lucy took off her heels and began to walk along the sand, feeling more lost than she had felt in a long time.

When her phone rang, she almost dropped her phone in the water. Expecting to see Gwen's name, she was surprised to see it was her sister, Thea, requesting a video call.

"Lucy!" said Thea. At the moment, Lucy could only see what looked like Thea's living room.

"Thea, you need to turn the camera."

"Shit, I thought I did." A second later, Thea's face appeared. "Can you see me?"

"Yeah." Lucy's smile wobbled.

She hadn't realized how much she needed some sisterly advice right now. Five years older than Lucy, Thea had taken care of the entire family, along with their oldest brother,

Trent, after their mother had died and their father had basically disengaged from the family. Thea worked as a graphic novelist, her series of comics recently published through the publishing press she and her boyfriend Anthony had started together. Irreverent yet pigheaded, Thea had hated Anthony until they'd both realized that they were actually perfect for each other.

"Where are you? Are you outside?" said Thea. "Do I hear the ocean?"

"I'm at the beach." Her voice broke, the tears overflowing now.

"Lucy, what happened? Why are you alone on the beach at night? It has to be freezing. Do I need to come up there and kick somebody's ass? Last time we texted, you sounded like you were having fun."

"I was!" wailed Lucy as she sat down on the sand, not caring about her nice dress. "Everything was going perfectly, and then it went to shit. I've ruined everything."

"Did you get fired?"

At that, Lucy scowled. "Of course not."

"Okay, well, just making sure." Thea turned her head. "I'm talking to Lucy. Say hi." A male voice rumbled something that sounded like hello. "Anthony says hi, by the way."

At the mention of Anthony, Lucy thought of Carter, and her tears started all over again. She was so mixed up inside. When had everything gotten so complicated?

"Did you get fired?" said Anthony, his face on the screen now.

Lucy had always found her sister's boyfriend rather intimidating, with his dark eyes and piercing gaze. He hadn't become one of the richest men in the country by being friendly. But he was devoted to Thea, so he must have a warm, squishy heart somewhere inside him.

"Why does everyone keep asking me that? No!" said Lucy.

"Wait, aren't you her boss?" said Thea to Anthony. "You'd be the one firing her."

"I'm not her direct supervisor, no. And anyway, the SAG rules make it tricky to fire actors, so she would've had to do something really stupid."

"Wow, Tony-kins, you're so helpful." Thea patted him on the cheek. "Go make me a sandwich and be useful for once."

Anthony whispered something in her ear that made her blush before he said, "Bye, Lucy. Good luck with whatever it is."

"Okay, he's gone. Now, tell me what happened," said Thea firmly.

"Anthony's not listening to this?"

Thea shook her head. "Spill."

It took a while, but Lucy managed to tell the entire sordid tale to Thea without sobbing too much. She told Thea about her crush on Hayden; how Carter had made a bargain with her to make Hayden jealous; and how things with Carter had turned into something that felt way too real for comfort.

"And now Hayden hates me, and Carter hates me, and I want to go home," she cried. She sounded like a child, but she didn't care. Sometimes you needed to cry your eyes out until you exhausted the angry child inside you.

"Oh, Luce. You've gotten yourself into quite a pickle." Thea sighed. "But I can't judge you, because God knows I've done some stupid things. What do you want to do?"

"That's just it: I don't know." Lucy wrapped her arm around her knees, shivering now against the cold. She hadn't felt it after her walk. "But even if I'm attracted to Carter, I know he's not the right one for me. I've heard all these things about him—"

"What things?" This was from Anthony, who had returned.

Lucy flushed to her hairline. "Thea, you said he wasn't listening!"

"He wasn't. But he must've been eavesdropping." Thea scowled at her boyfriend. "Stop upsetting my sister!"

"I'm not. But I know Carter better than anyone else. I can tell you if what you've heard is true or not." Anthony narrowed his eyes at Lucy. "Did you seriously agree to be his fake girlfriend?"

"Stop being judgy, Tony-Bunches-of-Oats. It's not a good look on you," said Thea.

"Will you stop calling me stupid nicknames?"

Thea batted her lashes. "Sorry, Tony-kins."

There was a brief tussle that made Lucy roll her eyes. Finally, both returned to the phone, Thea out of breath and Anthony's hair rumpled.

"If you guys want me to call later…" said Lucy.

"No, no, I want to hear the dirt. Then Anthony can confirm or deny," said Thea.

Lucy told the story that Hayden had relayed to her, regarding Carter and his ex-girlfriend Rosie. How Carter had not only cheated on Rosie, but he'd harassed her, too. As Lucy recounted the story, though, every word she uttered caused a pang inside her.

A second after Lucy had finished speaking, Anthony said bluntly, "That's a load of horseshit."

Lucy flushed, like she'd been the one to make up the story. "How do you know for sure?"

"Because I can tell you that Rosie cheated on *him*. She left him for that slimy son of a bitch—whatever his name is—and he was a total dick about it." Anthony scowled. "Look, I'm not going to tell you Carter is a saint. He isn't, and he'd agree with the assessment. But anything Kayden or Jayden or whatever says about him is bullshit."

Lucy didn't know if she wanted to cry or dance. Cry, because she'd been stupid enough not to see through Hayden in the first place; dance, because maybe her fears about Carter had nothing to substantiate them.

"What are you doing out here?" said a voice only yards away from her.

Lucy's breath caught in her throat as Carter approached her. The moon shone behind him, making him seem like some kind of mythical creature.

"Who is that?" said Thea.

"I'll talk to you guys later. Thanks for the help." Lucy hung up right as Thea was protesting, and she knew she'd hear an earful tomorrow from her sister.

Lucy got up, closing the distance between her and Carter. "What are you doing here?" she whispered.

"I could ask you the same question." He took in her appearance, with her sandy dress and bare feet. His expression turned grim. "Is Hayden here?"

She let out a startled laugh, tears springing to her eyes. "No. God, no. I was at his place tonight, but I left. That's why I'm here."

"At the beach, at night. Wearing barely anything." Carter's eyes narrowed. "Did that asshole do something to you?"

When Lucy didn't reply for a long moment, Carter swore colorfully. He took her hand and began to stalk toward the road.

"What?" said Lucy. "Where are we going?"

"You're going back to the bed-and-breakfast. I'm going to kill that piece of shit. I should've done it ages ago."

By the time they got to Carter's car, Lucy tugged on his hand to make him stop moving. "You're not going to kill anyone." When Carter ignored her, she dug her nails into his palm to get his attention.

"Carter," she said more firmly.

He winced. "Your claws are sharp, little spitfire. You're gonna draw blood if you're not careful."

She let his hand go, not the least bit sorry. "Like I said: you're not killing anyone. Hayden didn't do anything to me. I wanted to leave."

"And why did you want to leave?" Carter's voice was like velvet. He closed the smidge of distance between them until his hip brushed her belly. "Why did you leave your date with your Prince Charming?"

She licked her suddenly dry lips. "He's not my Prince Charming."

"You sure made a good show of it."

"He kissed me tonight." When Carter scowled, she caught his hand. "Don't freak out. I needed him to kiss me."

"Now I don't know who to be pissed off at," he said dryly.

"I realized that he wasn't the one I wanted to be kissing." She struggled to catch her breath, her heart fluttering like mad. Carter's gaze seemed endless, heated, a caress that she could almost feel.

He reached out and caressed her jaw. "Then who did you want to kiss?" His voice was rough.

"It was you. You, Carter," she burst out. "I don't even like you! This whole thing we started, it's gotten so complicated—"

"Little spitfire, do me a favor." He cupped her neck.

"What?"

"Shut up."

He swooped in and kissed her, and in that moment, Lucy knew. She *knew*. Moaning, she clung to him, practically melting at his feet. Her bones turned to liquid. Carter consumed every sense: smell, taste, touch, sight, sound. He was the center of her universe.

It terrified her.

"Baby, I need you," he groaned, and she could feel the evidence of his arousal against her belly. "Tell me you'll come back with me. I don't give a rat's ass if this is a shit idea. You've been driving me crazy since the second you insulted me that first day."

In response, she stood on her tiptoes and licked at the pulse in his neck. "I want you," she whispered.

Carter swore. "I was going to take you nice and slow in a bed like a good guy, but fuck it, I'm not driving even two miles and waiting that long." His smile was slow and heated. "Get in the backseat, little spitfire."

CHAPTER THIRTEEN

The last time Carter had made out with a woman in the backseat of his car, he had been fifteen, a virgin, and had come in his jeans within five minutes. It hadn't been his greatest shining moment.

Now, though, he wanted to savor Lucy. She made the most delicious little sounds in the back of her throat, like she couldn't get enough of him. He was infinitely glad that he'd sprung for a sports car that had a roomy backseat.

A tiny part of his mind whispered he should tell her the truth, but he pushed the thought away. It would only hurt her, and besides, things had changed. It was no longer about getting revenge on Hayden: it was all about Lucy and how she'd taken over his entire world in such a short time.

It was dim inside, but there was enough light from the distant streetlamps to let him see what he was doing. A small part of him wished he could see every inch of Lucy in vivid detail, but there would be other times for that. Right now, he needed to be inside her, to feel her shake and moan his name.

"Carter," she whispered, her hands pressing against his chest like a cat's paws. "What are we doing?"

He licked at the pulse point in her throat. "Do I have to explain the birds and the bees to you?" he teased.

"You're annoying. No, I mean—" She whimpered when he touched her breast through her dress. "I mean, where is this going?"

"Lucy." Carter practically growled the word. "Do you remember what I said to you earlier?" Before she could answer, he said, "Shut up and enjoy."

She hissed, offended, but any protests she might've been coming up with melted away when he reached under the hem of her silky dress to touch her even silkier inner thighs. She clenched her thighs around his hand even as she clung more tightly to him. She was like a vine trying to wrap around him, her need so obvious that it only stoked his own further.

When he got to the panel of her lace panties and found her already soaked, he groaned. "You need me that much, babe?"

She gasped when he pushed her panties to the side and slicked a finger through her wet folds. Her nails dug into his skin, and the bite of pain only egged him on.

"If I'd known you were that desperate for me," he said into her ear as he played with her, "I would've made you come with my hands and my mouth weeks ago. Maybe it would've made you less grumpy around me."

"No, it wouldn't have." Her continued gasping belied her words. "Oh my God, Carter, I'm so close." She bucked against his hand as he began to rub her clit in firm circles. God, he wished he could see her right now, pink and pretty and wet for him. But the sounds she made along with the feeling of her were erotic enough. His cock was already so hard it bordered on pain.

He slipped a finger inside her, rubbing her faster, until she let out a screech and convulsed against him. Growling, he captured her mouth in a hard kiss as he worked her through her release.

She was loose-limbed and happy after that, almost purring like a cat. "I want to feel you," she whispered as her hot little hands unbuckled his belt and dove inside his jeans. When she freed his cock and squeezed him at the base, he gritted his teeth to keep from coming right then and there like he had when he was fifteen years old.

This woman made him feel like he'd never slept with anyone else. It was only her, with her sweet mouth kissing his chest and her hands working his cock. Sweat beaded on his brow.

When he couldn't take it any longer, he reached for his wallet in his back pocket, pulling out a condom. He could feel Lucy's smile even in the dim light.

"So prepared," she said with a giggle. "Should I be offended?"

"You should be flattered. I never carry condoms in my wallet like some desperate loser." He rolled the latex on before lying down, pulling Lucy on top of him.

She pushed his shirt up and kissed his belly. "I'm not sure that's any better."

"What's any better?" He'd already forgotten what they were talking about.

Lucy nipped at the skin at his hip. "I'll explain later."

"You're a fucking brat." The words came out in a tone of amazement, especially as Lucy sank down on his cock, sheathing him in her tightness. He dug his fingers into her hips, forcing himself not to pound into her and taking control.

"You're an asshole," she countered as she began to ride him. Carter reached up and freed her breasts. Watching them bounce as she bounced on his cock almost made him lose it right then and there.

"Yet you're fucking me anyway." He leaned up and bit her bottom lip lightly. "So what does that say about you?"

"That I have low standards?" Her voice was breathless.

He bucked up into her, and she squealed. Grabbing her ass, he decided to take control. Lucy didn't protest as he thrust inside her, harder and harder, their bodies slapping against the leather seats. The windows even steamed up, and Carter would've cracked a joke about it if he weren't so close to his own release.

"You're gonna come for me again, because no matter your standards, I'm the only man who's ever made you feel like this," he rasped.

She opened her mouth to protest, but he reached down and began to rub her clit again. He felt her clench around him; she tipped her head back, completely surrendering to him.

When she came a second time, she screamed, so loudly that he had to cover her mouth with his hand. He chuckled darkly before groaning as his own orgasm hit him like a tidal wave. Emptying himself inside her, he was pretty sure he'd died, and he wasn't the least bit bothered by that fact.

Lucy collapsed on top of him even as she kissed him. His heart caught in his throat, but he pushed the feeling aside. This was just sex and nothing else.

Eventually, they cleaned themselves up as much as they

could in the confines of a car. It took a while, only because Carter kept kissing Lucy, making her giggle and playfully push him away.

"Man, we pulled a *Titanic*," said Lucy, looking at the still-steamed windows. She drew a smiley face with her finger. "I'm seriously impressed."

"Probably a good thing. These windows aren't tinted, so anyone could've seen us."

She whirled on him. "What? Oh God, I didn't even notice. What if someone walked past—?"

Carter snaked an arm around her. "We're in the middle of nowhere at…what time is it? Midnight?" He kissed her ear. "Come back to my room with me."

He waited for her answer with bated breath. The last time he'd let a woman stay the night was eons ago. He preferred a quick fuck followed by an equally quick exit.

"I probably shouldn't," she said finally, "but I don't think this night is about making good decisions."

He'd parse that response later. Kissing her one last time, he climbed out of the car, groaning as his muscles—particularly his shoulder—protested. God, he was too old for this shit.

The second Carter locked his room's door at the bed-and-breakfast, he pulled Lucy into his arms, lifting her up until her feet dangled off the floor. She laughed and wrapped her legs around his waist.

"I should go change," she whispered.

"Why? You're just going to be naked again."

He'd turned on a lamp, and he could finally see her face: her soft eyes, her kiss-bruised lips, the flush on her cheeks. Her hair was a mess, and his lips twitched when he saw that one of the straps on her dress was twisted up.

She looked absolutely beautiful.

"You're so practical," she said.

"When it comes to getting a woman naked, I'm always practical. Logical. All those things."

She smiled, and he thought it was the first smile she'd given him that wasn't tinged with annoyance. Her usual barbs had faded away, and he suddenly wanted to keep this side of Lucy completely to himself. The side of her that was sweet and giving and lovely.

When he took her mouth, he made the kiss slow and tender. She ran her fingers through his hair in gentle strokes. His heart slammed in his chest again even as his cock came back to attention.

Not wanting to think about all the strange emotions rolling through him, he promptly tossed her onto his bed and climbed over her, letting desire wash away everything but the feeling of being deep inside his little spitfire.

DESPITE HER EXHAUSTION and the fact that her body currently felt like mush, Lucy couldn't sleep. Carter, for his part, was snoring softly next to her. He'd fallen asleep within minutes after the second time they'd had sex, but not before he'd thrown an arm over her and pulled her close.

Lucy sighed softly. It was still dark out, but it had to be close to dawn. Squinting at the alarm clock, she realized that she had three hours before she had to get ready for filming.

Her stomach rumbled, but it would be a few hours before she could get breakfast downstairs. She considered pilfering something from the kitchen and asking Gwen for forgiveness later.

Carter grunted in his sleep. Lucy bit her lip to keep from laughing.

There was some light coming through the curtains, which let her watch his face as he slept. He was more relaxed, the intensity that drove him having melted away. She reached up and brushed a lock of hair from his forehead.

Food. She needed food. Pushing Carter's arm away and hoping she didn't wake him, she dressed hastily, stuffing her panties and bra into her purse. She was only going down the hallway, and it was unlikely anyone was awake at this hour.

She tiptoed out of Carter's room, purse and heels in her hand. When an indrawn gasp behind her made her start, she barely kept from dropping everything onto the floor in a loud clatter.

"Lucy!"

Lucy blushed to the roots of her hair as she turned to see Gwen standing only a few yards away on the stairs. Gwen cocked an eyebrow as she waited for Lucy's explanation.

Not knowing what to say, Lucy shrugged. "It's a long story."

"I bet it is. And although I'm tempted to get you to spill it right now, I'm going back to bed."

"Were you with someone, too?" Lucy asked hopefully.

Gwen snorted. "I was hungry, and I heard a door open. When I saw it was you coming out of Carter Roberts's room…"

"Okay, okay. I need to go to my room." Before Gwen turned to go, Lucy said, "Can I get some food from the kitchen? I'll pay you back."

"No need. Your payment will be telling me the dirty details of what happened tonight." Gwen smiled like a cat and waved airily as she returned downstairs.

Lucy hurried to her room, where she washed her face, brushed her teeth, and put on a tank and yoga pants. After she brushed her hair, which was a tangled mess that somehow had sand in it, she put on her slippers to go downstairs. As the stairs creaked with each step, she winced, hoping she didn't wake anyone up. She didn't need anyone questioning her about why she was lurking around in the early-morning hours.

When she entered the kitchen, she flipped on the light over the oven and began to make herself a cup of tea. She found some leftover pastries and began to devour one before her tea was even finished brewing.

"Did you even chew that before you swallowed?" said Carter, his smile warm and teasing.

"I'm starving," she said through a mouthful of food. "I had oysters with Hayden…"

She trailed off, blushing furiously. God, she'd forgotten all about Hayden and their terrible date. And she had to film with him today. Her stomach twisted at the thought, and suddenly the pastry that had tasted so good was like ash in her mouth.

Fear curdled inside her, fear that Hayden would be petty enough to use her rejection of him against her. Memories of Glen and his retribution when she'd told him no came back with painful force.

The kettle whistled, but the sound barely registered. It was only when Carter began pouring them both a cup of tea that she realized she'd been far away.

"You look like you're going to puke," said Carter bluntly.

He pushed the mug of tea toward her before setting a stool down next to her. "Sit before you faint."

"I told you before: I never faint," she grumbled. She sighed as she sat down. "And I'm not going to puke."

Carter leaned on the large kitchen island, his forearms bulging. He bit into a bear claw with gusto. Lucy waited for him to ask more questions, but he munched on his pastry as if he didn't have a care in the world.

She began to pick apart her cheese Danish until it was a pile of flaky crumbs. "Do you think I'm easy?" she blurted.

The expression on Carter's face made her wish she hadn't said anything.

"Never mind. Don't answer that. It was a stupid question," she said.

"It was a stupid question, because you're the least *easy* woman I've ever met." Carter snorted. "Easy? The fact I got into your pants is a small miracle. You acted like that shop was closed for business, ignoring whatever you were doing with what's-his-face."

She moaned. "God, I was so stupid, and now Hayden hates me. How are we going to keep working together?" She gripped her tea mug so hard her fingers hurt. "He could blackball me in Hollywood. One word in the right person's ear—"

"Lucy." Carter turned her so she faced him and tilted her chin up. "Do you regret what happened between us last night?" were his soft words.

Even though his touch was gentle, she could feel the strength in his fingers. "Of course not."

"You never wanted Hayden?" His fingers gripped her chin —not enough to hurt, but enough that she couldn't move.

"No," she said, her voice breathy. "It was always you. I was just lying to myself."

"Then if he somehow decides to be a petty piece of shit and spread rumors, you'll have to fight back. He doesn't get to do that to you because you told him no."

Carter let go of her chin, and Lucy rested her head on his chest, his heartbeat a soothing rhythm against her ear.

"I almost quit acting, you know," she said, closing her eyes. "The only reason I didn't was because I got this role. And now look what happened."

"Tell me."

With a sigh, Lucy told Carter about Glen and how he'd made her life hell through all the months she'd worked at his theater. Carter said nothing, but she could feel the tension in his body as she spoke.

"I should've been tougher with him. If I'd told him from the start what he was doing wasn't okay, he wouldn't have kept trying. I led him on." She was practically babbling at this point.

"No, babe." Carter made her look up at him again. She caught her breath as she saw the barely restrained anger in his expression. "He was your boss and he took advantage of that. A real man doesn't force himself on a woman. He was a sniveling jackass with a tiny dick."

Lucy let out the breath she'd been holding. She didn't know why it mattered so much, but having Carter defend her and tell her that what had happened with Glen wasn't her fault meant more than she could say. A lump formed in her throat.

"I didn't tell anyone about that," she said softly, "not even my family. They're already convinced I should go home. My brothers would've come down to LA and killed Glen."

"I'm glad you didn't tell them, because I'll kill him myself."

Lucy almost laughed, but it died in her throat when she realized Carter was serious. Her heart bubbled over, and she couldn't stop herself from bringing his head down and kissing him.

His reaction was instantaneous: he thrust his tongue into her mouth, claiming her without apology. Heat sparked inside her, starting low in her belly.

"It wasn't your fault," said Carter as he brushed a lock of hair from her cheek. "And if Hayden tries anything, I'll break his kneecaps."

"I don't generally advocate violence, but I wouldn't mind seeing that. He was a dick to me last night."

Carter growled, vowing revenge, but Lucy hushed him with another kiss. It was only when they heard footsteps outside the kitchen that they pulled apart.

"Go up to my room. I'll follow you in a minute," said Carter.

"Who says I want to go to your room?"

He smiled, that feral smile that made her heart stop. "I can fuck you here if you want. I'm not picky."

"I think that'd be unsanitary." Her words were breathless as she snagged a pastry and scampered upstairs before Carter made good on his threat.

CHAPTER FOURTEEN

Carter helped Lucy up the embankment until they both stood on the cliff that overlooked the sound. It was the highest point in Hazel Island—not Mount Everest, but enough of a hike to get his blood thrumming—and it was one of those perfect summer days that reminded you why you put up with the winter here in Washington State. Lucy inhaled deeply and took his arm.

Everything was emerald green, moss growing in pockets down the cliffside. Seagulls cawed and circled in the sky, a few skimming the water to catch unsuspecting fish. Without the clang of the city or the traffic, Carter could imagine this place was far away from everything that wanted to sink its claws into him. He could almost imagine his shoulder didn't hurt or that this thing with Lucy could last beyond the summer.

"I could live here," breathed Lucy as she entwined her fingers with his.

"Really?" He considered. "I think I'd get bored after a while."

"I was raised in Fair Haven, so I'm used to small towns. I

like them. Everyone knows you, you don't have the traffic, the rent is affordable… nothing like LA. The first year I lived there, I thought I'd die if I drove on the highway."

"All very practical points, little spitfire. Good thing I'm not worried about paying my rent."

She wrinkled her nose at him. "Oh, lord your wealth over a poor peasant like me. How about you show me your bank balance while you're at it?"

"I save that for the third date." He smacked her ass, which made her squeal.

"I'm surprised you don't do it first thing." She widened her eyes. "Just in case you aren't impressive in any other areas."

"Brat." That remark made him pick her up and swing her over his shoulder. She laughed between her protests as he carried her down the hill. She hardly weighed more than a hundred pounds, and as tiny as she was, he could've carried her back to Seattle if he'd had a mind to.

"Are you going to throw me off a cliff? Let me go!" She poked at his lower back and pulled at his shirt like some kind of busy raccoon scrounging for trash.

He patted her ass and kept walking, ignoring her attempts to kick him in the face.

He had no particular destination in mind, but he realized he was going to have to put her down simply because his shoulder was starting to ache. He'd used his right hand without even thinking about it. Stupid mistake. He couldn't stop the wince as he set her down on the ground.

"Was I that heavy?" Lucy's eyes widened. "Oh my God, that's your injured shoulder! I shouldn't have let you carry me like that. Are you okay?"

Normally he hated when people tried to coddle him,

acting like he was going to break, but he didn't mind Lucy's touching him. It helped that she smelled amazing and her breasts were pressed against his side, reminding him of why he liked her so much.

"I'm fine." He took a few steps and felt dizzy at the sudden rush of pain down his arm. *Damn damn damn.* He'd been so wrapped up in Lucy that he simply hadn't been thinking.

They were currently on a deserted trail that had led them up the cliff. Carter guessed they were about two miles from where he'd parked. He could see a few tourists wandering the trail that led into a nature reserve, but it was pretty much deserted around here.

"Come on." Lucy took his arm and guided him down the path until they entered the forest. The pine trees here were at least one hundred feet tall, making the forest dappled with sunshine and moving shadows. Pinecones and needles crunched under their feet, the spicy scent of them oddly soothing.

"Here we go." Lucy made him sit down on a bench before she sat next to him. "You're really pale." She touched his forehead, where a light sheen of sweat had broken out.

He felt, in a word, like shit. He'd been given painkillers, but he hated how out of it they made him feel. It was only when the pain became unbearable that he'd give in and take one. But he didn't exactly bring them along on hikes in case he was stupid enough to throw a grown woman over his bum shoulder.

Lucy didn't say anything, but simply sat with him. He couldn't remember the last time anyone had done that with him. His dad certainly hadn't. Some of his fellow players had visited him in the hospital after his surgery, but they'd had their own lives to deal with.

"Do I need to go back for the car?" said Lucy after a while.

"You can't exactly drive it up here, babe."

"I could try."

Looking at her expression, he had a feeling she would try. That realization, that she would do that for him, made something inside him twist. He felt guilty, confused, but most of all amazed that she'd become an integral part of him so quickly. He only wondered how he'd manage to end this by the time this gig was over.

Why end it? his mind asked.

Because they were in different worlds. Because he wasn't into commitment. Because he'd lied to her from the beginning and he was too much of a fucking coward to tell her the truth. Because he knew that things like this never lasted in the long run.

Eventually, the pain changed into a dull ache, although if he lifted his shoulder or arm, it hurt like a bitch.

"How did it happen?" said Lucy.

He knew what she meant, but he was tempted to play dumb. The memories always lurked in the back of his mind. It was only then that he realized he hadn't had dreamed about his injury since that night weeks ago.

"I was fucking stupid," he said bluntly, "and I wasn't thinking. I was practicing and my shoulder was hurting, but I kept pushing myself. It was like if I didn't, nothing that I had done mattered. And then…" He shrugged, then grimaced. Apparently shrugging wasn't an option either.

"When do you find out if you can play or not?"

"In a few weeks, I'll have to go back to Seattle for an appointment. Basically it's my surgeon's call."

Lucy's brow furrowed. "What happens if you have to retire? What'll you do?"

"How the hell do I know?" he snapped. Lucy flinched, and guilt immediately flooded him. "Sorry, babe. I don't know if I have an answer to that question because fuck if I know. I mean, I won't starve, and I would've retired eventually. But to have it end like this, before I'd done everything I'd wanted…"

"I get it," she said softly. "When your identity is wrapped up in the one thing you know how to do. I didn't want to give up acting even when I thought I'd be better off because I don't know how to be anything else. Who am I if I'm not acting? Just Lucy, the girl who failed at doing the one thing she wanted to do."

His breath caught, only because Lucy was the first person to understand that need inside him, to prove himself to the world. He'd never understood people who could float through life without an ambition to drive them.

"It'd be one thing if you'd played until you decided you were done. Having that decision taken from you is different," she said. Her smile was sad, and Carter almost couldn't take the understanding in her gaze. It made him want to push her away, because if he wasn't careful, she'd reach inside his chest and take his heart for her own.

Because he didn't know what else to do, he kissed her. She reacted with surprise, but it didn't take long for her to respond in kind. She tasted like the dappled sunshine surrounding them. He barely restrained himself from pulling her onto his lap and having her right here on a bench in the middle of a park. It was only when they heard footsteps that they parted, both breathless when a couple walked past them.

"Are you up for a walk?" said Lucy. "I've wanted to walk this trail since I got here, I just hadn't gotten around to it."

"I'll manage."

She shot him a shrewd look, like she didn't believe him.

"I'm fine," he said. He got up, lifted his shoulder, and managed to keep himself from wincing at the burning pain that resulted.

"If we need to go back—"

"No." His tone was hard now. "I'm fine."

This time, Lucy didn't take his hand.

OUT OF THE corner of her eye, Lucy kept tabs on Carter, waiting for him to give in and say they should go back to the car. They had another two miles to walk to get to the car in the first place. But she also knew she couldn't stop a stubborn man from being determined to prove he was infallible. *Men,* she thought in exasperation. *He'd be bleeding out and he wouldn't tell me he was hurting.*

When he stepped hard on an unexpected dip in the trail, he winced. Lucy stopped walking.

"We're going back," she said. "You're going to push yourself too hard again."

"Stop coddling me," he growled.

"I'm not coddling you. I'm trying to keep you from hurting yourself again."

His expression was more savage than she'd ever seen it.

"You're not my mother. You're not even my fucking girlfriend."

It was like an arrow straight to her heart. Her bottom lip wobbled, but she managed to say in an even voice, "You're right. So if you want to keep hurting yourself, go right ahead. I won't stop you."

She walked away, not caring if Carter followed. He'd driven them here, but she'd catch a ride with someone back to town. She'd walk back to town if she had to. It wasn't like she hadn't done it before.

You're not even my fucking girlfriend. She'd known that, of course, but now she wondered if she was anything to Carter except a fling. She'd told herself that she wouldn't let her heart get involved, but based on how much it hurt right now, she was involved. Too involved for her own good.

"Lucy. Dammit, Lucy, wait." Carter caught her by the arm. "I shouldn't have said that."

She whirled on him, wrenching her arm away. "What am I to you, then? Just an easy lay? A fuck buddy? What term would you like to use, Mr. Roberts?"

"I don't fucking know. And I know you don't either. This wasn't exactly something I planned."

"Do you think I'd planned this either?" She wanted to shake him.

Pushing his fingers through his hair, he sighed heavily. "Look, let's be honest with each other. You're going back to LA after this; I'm going back to Seattle. Why can't we just enjoy each other while we can?"

Ice climbed down Lucy's spine, her stomach rolling. She shouldn't have expected a different answer, but it hurt all the same. Did she want Carter to tell her he wanted to make this work, that he cared about her? That, God forbid, he was in love with her?

Her mind in tumult, she didn't know what she wanted anymore, except that the thought of this ending in a few weeks made her want to cry. Swallowing against tears, she said, "You're right. I wasn't expecting anything else, either. So we might as well stop fighting since our time is limited."

She was glad, once again, that she was an actress, because it took all of her talent to keep from bursting into tears when she saw the relief on Carter's face.

They hiked back to the car in silence, which allowed Lucy to order her thoughts. She couldn't get mad at Carter for thinking this…thing that they had wasn't going to be more. She would've thought the same. She was madder at herself for wanting it to become more.

By the time they returned to the bed-and-breakfast, it was late afternoon. Carter walked her to her door and shoved his hands into his pockets.

"I'll see you tonight?" he said, his expression heated.

Knowing she was a sucker and an idiot, she nodded, knowing full well that no other man had put her heart in as much jeopardy as this one.

CHAPTER FIFTEEN

The following Monday, Carter woke up at five a.m. and couldn't go back to sleep. He considered waking Lucy as well, but she was currently wrapped up in the blankets, cocooned in warmth. She was fast asleep, and he didn't have the heart to wake her. Besides, he'd be back within an hour.

He dressed in his running clothes and headed out. The town was still, fog rolling in from the water, and it was so quiet that the only sounds were Carter's exhalations and the sound of his tennis shoes against the pavement.

He had two weeks until he had to go to Seattle for his appointment with his orthopedic surgeon. Lately, he'd dreamt of the appointment, and one night he'd tossed and turned until Lucy had had to wake him up. The dreams always ended with him being told that he was officially retired for good, and it only increased the ball of anxiety building in his gut.

Was that why he was so obsessed with Lucy? Because she distracted him from what could very well happen? It made sense, but then again, he was always the kind of guy who got bored with a woman after a night or two. Then he'd find another one that would come to his bed, and another. It didn't really matter who the woman was, and the women never cared about him, either. It had worked for him—until now.

Lucy was like a fever in his blood. He couldn't get enough of her. He'd thought if he slept with her once, that would be that. He'd move on and find someone else. But it had only made it worse. She haunted him, and every day that she had to leave for filming, he wanted to lock her up with him in his room and never let her out.

Obviously he was losing his damn mind. That was the only explanation. Next he'd turn into the type of guy who bought an engagement ring on the third date and cried at Hallmark movies.

A half hour later, Carter turned to begin his run back to the bed-and-breakfast. Lucy would most likely be awake by the time he arrived, but they'd probably have time for a quickie before she had to go film. Anticipation built inside him. The thought of Lucy naked in the morning sunshine was enough to make him sprint.

About two blocks from the bed-and-breakfast, Hayden stepped out of Dee's Coffee Shop. Carter had no intention of stopping to chat, but Hayden said in a suspiciously cheery voice, "Good morning."

Lucy had told Carter all about her date with Hayden and the subsequent awkwardness between them during filming. Carter had been watching the actor, making sure he didn't do anything that would upset Lucy. If Hayden so much as sneezed in her direction, Carter would pummel him into the sidewalk.

"Have a nice run?" Hayden squinted up at the sky. "It's going to get pretty warm today, I think."

Carter scowled. The fuck was he talking about? "Did you stop me to talk about the weather?"

Hayden ignored him. "I actually was just talking to Rosie. Remember her? I told her I wasn't interested anymore, but she keeps wanting me back." He sighed and shook his head. "Was she like that when you fucked her? Before she met me, obviously."

"No. But then she did a lot of things I hadn't expected after she met you."

"Touché. But now you got your revenge." Hayden spread his fingers, his smile devoid of warmth. "You stole little Lucy right out from under my nose. Did you fuck her yet? Based on the look on your face, you did."

Carter didn't think: he grabbed Hayden by his collar, his coffee spilling onto the sidewalk, and slammed him against the brick wall of the coffee shop.

"If you so much as look at her the wrong way, I'll fucking kill you," growled Carter. He gripped Hayden's collar tighter, until the actor turned a little blue.

"You seriously think you have the higher moral ground here?" Hayden gasped. "When we both know you only fucked her to get revenge?"

Carter paled, but it only made Hayden laugh. His laugh turned into another gasp as Carter shook him and finally let him go.

"You don't know a damn thing. Stay away from her, you hear me? Otherwise I'll get your ass fired," said Carter.

Hayden rubbed his throat, scowling. His usually perfectly coifed hair was disheveled, and his coffee had landed on his left pant leg, staining it to the knee. "You're going to a lot of trouble for somebody who's just an easy slut," he spat.

Carter punched him in the gut. Hayden collapsed at his feet, wheezing, and the only reason he didn't punch the asshole a second time was because he didn't feel like going to jail that day while Hayden walked free.

"You touch her, and you're dead. Got it, Masterson? I'm not fucking playing."

Hayden looked up at him, his gaze full of hatred. "You'll regret this."

When Carter arrived back at the bed-and-breakfast, Lucy was awake and waiting for him in the dining room. "Where have you been?" she asked, smiling, but the smile faded as she saw his expression. "Did something happen?"

Carter didn't care that other people were watching. Wrapping an arm around her, he kissed her forehead. "Nothing. I took a detour that took longer than I expected." He then murmured in her ear, "Come upstairs and take a shower with me."

Her cheeks turned pink. "I already took a shower," she said primly.

"Come upstairs anyway."

She glanced at the clock on the wall. "If I say yes, you have to promise not to mess up my hair. And be quick."

"Get your ass upstairs before I carry you up there, woman. And I'll take all the time I want."

"Pushy, pushy." She stuck out her tongue, smiling, and Carter knew right then that he was done for.

FILMING CONTINUED, despite the tension that Lucy felt every time she was around Hayden. He never mentioned their ill-fated date. If she hadn't been paying attention, she would've thought he'd forgotten all about it. But sometimes she detected an antipathy he radiated toward her, though he always masked it with a smile. Sometimes she wondered if she was imagining things. He hadn't actually done anything to her since that night, and she was glad that at least on the surface, it had been brushed under the rug.

The Saturday before Carter left Hazel Island for Seattle, Lucy was invited out for drinks with Gwen. Alex joined them; Felicity had been invited, but according to Gwen, it had been a small miracle that they'd gotten her to leave her house to come to the beach, let alone go out with them all a second time that summer.

"Felicity is the most private person I've ever known," said Gwen, shrugging. "But I keep inviting her to things in the hopes that she'll say yes."

"You're one of those people, aren't you?" Alex's smile was wry. "You remind me of my sister. She'll browbeat you into hanging out with her. I'd rather not beg someone to hang out with me."

"It's not about begging, it's about making sure people feel like they're invited to come along even if they don't want to," said Gwen.

Lucy was only paying partial attention to their conversation. Her mind was solely on Carter. He'd become edgier, more distant in the last few days with his appointment looming before him. She'd tried to get him to talk about it, but he'd shut her out so many times that she'd given up. That hadn't stopped her from going to his room every night. She'd still wanted to feel connected to him, and if sex was the only way, so be it.

But deep down inside, she knew this thing between them was coming to an end. More than likely, Carter wouldn't return to Hazel Island with only another week of filming left. He'd return to his life, and soon, Lucy would return to LA. The thought of never seeing Carter again made her want to drown her sorrows in a large bottle of wine.

"Lucy, what do you think?" said Gwen, interrupting Lucy's train of thought.

Lucy forced her thoughts to the present. "What do I think about what?"

"This is why I don't hang out with people who have new boyfriends. They're always distracted. If they're not texting their boyfriends, they're totally out of it." Alex wrinkled her nose. "No offense, Luce."

"If you're talking about me," said Lucy, "Carter isn't my boyfriend. So you don't have to worry about that."

Since the first time that Lucy had met her, Alex was speechless. She gaped at Lucy, then at Gwen, before saying, "Are you serious? You guys are ridiculous together."

Alex winced after something collided with her leg—the likely culprit being Gwen's foot.

"Don't kick me. You know I'm right." Alex pointed her finger in Lucy's face. "That guy looks at you like you hung the moon in the sky. It's nauseating. It's like something out of a romance novel."

"Alex, don't torture Lucy," said Gwen in exasperation. Gwen tilted her head toward Lucy. "That being said, you never did spill the beans. Considering you had a date with Hayden and ended up in Carter's room that same night."

Alex choked on her beer, Gwen pounding her on the back. Lucy blushed scarlet.

"Oh my God, you're my hero," gasped Alex. "You're dating them both?"

"What? No, no. I'm not."

Gwen and Alex waited for an explanation, and Lucy finally told them everything: her disastrous date with Hayden; Carter finding her on the beach; and almost everything that had happened after that. Lucy didn't feel the need to tell them about their various sexual escapades, no matter how enjoyable they were.

"You banged Carter Roberts in his backseat? You really are my hero." Alex's eyes were practically sparkling. "High five!"

Lucy rolled her eyes but high-fived Alex anyway. Gwen's expression was devoid of any mirth: she looked more concerned than anything.

"But you're not dating. Is that what you want?" said Gwen in a soft voice.

Lucy's blood froze, the fear that had been building inside her only growing. Up until this point, she hadn't wanted to be honest with herself. It was easier to say that when this ended, she would be fine. Her heart hadn't been touched, so she wouldn't end up longing for a man she'd known she couldn't ever have.

"It doesn't matter, because he's going back to Seattle and to playing ball." Lucy shrugged, drawing circles in the condensation that had formed on the table. "It's just a fling."

Gwen sighed. "Honey, let me give you some advice. You know I was married, right? Well, I got divorced finally because I realized I wasn't going to be what my ex wanted me to be. And I can tell you right now, he never looked at me the way Carter looks at you. You might not see it, but I have. He looks like he doesn't know what to do with you, but he can't look away, either. He never takes his eyes off of you."

"How do you feel about him?" was Alex's question.

Lucy wanted to burst into tears. She forced herself to draw in a deep breath before she answered in a whisper, "I don't know."

"I think you do, but that would mean you'd have to do something about it," said Gwen kindly.

Lucy brushed away the tears that were threatening to fall. "I think—" She swallowed. "I think I want more than this with him. I think I'm falling in love with him."

Once she'd said the words, she felt both fear and a sense of freedom. Because Gwen was right: now that she'd admitted the truth, she owed it to herself—and to Carter—to be honest with him.

Gwen squeezed Lucy's hand. "Then you should tell him. Wouldn't you rather know than not?"

"Yeah, not being honest is one of the easiest ways to lose somebody you care about." Alex's voice was far away, and Lucy wondered who she was thinking about.

Lucy fell silent, her thoughts whirling. Gwen and Alex didn't ask her more questions, but simply sat in silent support of her. Once again, she couldn't help but be immensely grateful that she'd gotten to know these women this summer. At the very least, she'd have no regrets on that front.

When a man walked by their table, Gwen froze. It was imperceptible, but Lucy could almost see the tension running through Gwen's body. Lucy gazed more closely at the man: he was tall, his skin browned from the sun, his sandy brown hair streaked with blond. He had arms the size of barrels. Lucy realized that she'd seen him in town a few times, including when he'd dropped off a case of fresh crabs for the bed-and-breakfast.

The man's gaze caught Gwen's. He said in a rumbling voice, "Didn't know you came here."

Gwen didn't respond for a long moment, prompting Alex to reply for her. "It's the only decent dive bar in town, and you can always get a guy to buy us some drinks."

The man looked at Lucy. "You're one of the actors."

Gwen finally collected herself. "Jack, you haven't met Lucy yet? Lucy, this is Jack Benson. He's a fisherman and catches most of the seafood I use at the bed-and-breakfast. Nobody catches better crabs."

Jack looked embarrassed, and Gwen looked embarrassed, and Lucy desperately wanted to know what was between these two. But then Jack said goodbye and that was that.

Until the one bartender working brought them a tray of drinks. "From Jack," he said.

"Huh," said Alex, choosing one of the drinks for herself.

"Why are you surprised? Didn't you say guys always buy drinks for you here?" said Lucy.

Alex snorted. "Jack Benson never buys women drinks, and I've been to this bar many, many times. But I guess there's always an exception." She looked straight at Gwen as she said the words.

Gwen had nothing to say to that remark.

Gwen has a secret, thought Lucy, *and someday I'm going to get her to spill the beans.*

But not tonight, because Lucy had her own love life to deal with first.

CHAPTER SIXTEEN

Despite Lucy's best efforts, Carter eluded her all weekend. When she knocked on his door Friday night, he wasn't in. She texted him, but he only replied to say that he was busy and he'd call her.

He didn't call her.

She tried again on Sunday morning, but if he was in his room, he didn't feel like opening the door. She called him one last time, knowing that he was ghosting her already before he took off for Seattle. When he didn't pick up, she didn't leave a voicemail. He probably wouldn't listen to it anyway.

If Carter wanted to end things, he could say it to her face. She sat in her room all Sunday and listened for the sound of his footsteps coming up the stairs. She'd recognize them anywhere.

It was close to midnight when she heard the stairs creaking. Her eyes flew open; she'd fallen into a doze. Her heart in her throat, she heard whoever it was take a half dozen steps down the hallway before they stopped to unlock their door.

She threw open her door just in time to see Carter closing

his. Before she could jam her foot in the door, he locked it. The sound of the lock clicking felt like chains around her heart, squeezing painfully.

Lucy knocked. No answer. She knocked again, more loudly. "I'll keep knocking until I wake up everyone in this damn place," she said through the door. "Stop avoiding me, you coward."

Carter threw open the door so quickly she almost tumbled to the floor in front of him. He yanked her inside, and she could smell liquor on his breath. So, that was where he'd been: drinking and probably feeling sorry for himself again.

"Anyone ever tell you that you're a pain in the ass?" he grumbled.

"Only you. And if anyone is a pain in the ass, it's you. Why are you ignoring me?"

Carter picked up a glass of amber-colored liquor, swirling it around for a moment. When he looked up at Lucy, his gaze was stark. "I thought that was what you'd want. This was never going anywhere, Lucy."

"So you made the decision yourself without consulting me? Fuck you, Carter." She grabbed the glass from him and slammed it down onto a nearby table, the liquid sloshing onto the wooden surface. "Fuck you and whatever horse you rode in on. Do you think you're protecting me? Or are you just protecting yourself?"

"You don't want to do this," was his dark reply.

A little thrill burst inside her, but she wasn't afraid. She could see beneath the mask he put on, the mask that made him irreverent and charming, without a care in the world when everything was collapsing around him. She could see it because she could see the same thing in herself.

"You don't know what I want, because you haven't asked," she said.

He put his arm around her waist, pulling her close enough that she could feel how hard he was already. "What do you want, little spitfire?" His words were a heated whisper against his ear.

"You. It's always been you."

He sighed, like he wished she'd had another answer. Lucy, though, wasn't one to give up easily. Stepping away, she pulled his shirt off, her breath catching as she took in the marvel that was his bare chest and abdomen. She'd seen him naked plenty of times already, but she'd yet to get a chance to savor it. She skimmed a finger down the line that bisected his belly, watching as he sucked in a breath.

When she dipped her index finger below the waistband of his jeans, he cupped her head and kissed her. He gripped her hard, his mouth ruthless as he devoured her. Moaning, she clung to him, because otherwise she'd melt into a puddle at his feet.

"I was trying to do the right thing," he muttered, almost to himself. "I'm leaving tomorrow."

"I know."

"It'd be easier if we ended everything."

"Probably."

Lucy touched his cheek before leaning forward and kissing him over his heart. He groaned, saying her name, as she kneeled in front of him. He let go of her hair, as if to tell her she had a choice in the matter. It only made her want to do this more.

When she freed him from the confines of his jeans, she licked his cock from base to tip. He shuddered. Lucy had always been ambivalent about going down on a guy: he enjoyed it while she found it to be something of a chore.

But this was different. She was half Carter's size, yet she held the power now. As she sucked him, swirling her tongue around the tip, he gripped her ponytail but didn't make her go faster. Feeling the tension in his body, the way he grew harder with every lick and every squeeze of her hand around the base of his cock, only made her want him more.

She could feel him getting close when he gently pushed her away and lifted her to her feet. Soon, their clothes were discarded in heaps on the floor as they fell into Carter's bed.

"Fuck, baby, you're going to kill me," said Carter. "Your mouth should be illegal."

"You're welcome."

"Brat."

He nipped at her collarbone, squeezing her breasts together. He flicked her nipples until they were deliciously sensitive. When he parted her thighs and spread her sex, she bucked against his hand. She was already close, and he'd hardly touched her yet.

"I'm tempted to let you come right now, but I want it to be around my cock this time." Carter's words made her flush with want.

He moved off her for a brief moment, and she heard the sound of a foil packet opening before Carter rejoined her. He thrust inside her to the hilt, and Lucy's eyes rolled back inside her head.

He gave her no quarter. He pounded into her until he had to cover her mouth with his hand to keep her from waking up the entire bed-and-breakfast.

"Come for me, little spitfire. I want to feel it," he growled into her ear.

It only took another thrust and her release hit her, hard and fast and relentless. She bit Carter's palm, and it only made him laugh darkly as he came, too. The laugh turned into a tortured groan as he shuddered and slammed his fist into the mattress next to her head.

Lucy vaguely heard Carter get up, water running in the bathroom, until he returned. Her body was jelly, her heart pounding in her ears. Despite her exhaustion, she was wide awake.

How had she ever thought she wouldn't fall in love with him?

Because she realized with a sinking heart that she was stupidly, ridiculously, completely in love with him. And worst of all, he was leaving tomorrow and hadn't said a word about this continuing.

Lucy thought of Gwen's advice from three nights ago. Perhaps Carter felt the same way, but he wasn't sure of *her* feelings.

When he returned to the bed and wrapped her in his arms, she turned to face him. "What time are you leaving tomorrow?"

"Early. I have to catch the first ferry."

That meant she couldn't wait until morning to tell him. Gathering her courage, she said in a rush, "I love you."

He didn't react. She felt his fingers tighten on her hip, but otherwise, it was like he was made of stone.

"I didn't know until…just now." Lucy laughed, a little hysterical. "I know this thing we have has been weird and complicated—"

Carter cut her off. "Don't." He sounded anguished. "Just, don't."

Her heart fell to her toes. "What are you saying?"

"I'm leaving tomorrow." He kissed her forehead and added in a gentle voice, "Go to sleep. We can talk later."

The anxiety that had been building inside her abated. They'd talk later. That meant he saw something for them in the future. Hope filling her, she let herself be lulled to sleep in the safety of Carter's arms.

CHAPTER SEVENTEEN

When Carter stepped outside, fans mobbed him within minutes. Although most Seattleites were generally reticent to approach strangers, apparently today they made an exception for Carter. Fans of all ages crowded around him, demanding photos and autographs.

"When are you playing again?"

"You need to come back next season!"

"Were you here to see your doctor? What's the verdict?"

Carter ignored the questions, smiling for the cameras and signing so many autographs that his hand began to cramp. He finally made some excuse and pushed his way through the crowd.

He had no destination in mind. It didn't really matter where he went, because his career was officially over.

After multiple tests that included both X-rays and CT scans, Carter's orthopedic surgeon had declared that his torn rotator cuff hadn't healed to the extent it had needed to for him to return. *I know it's not what you wanted to hear*, he'd said in that calm doctor voice that Carter hated. *But it had been a real long shot anyway. I don't need to tell you that this is the worst injury any pitcher can get.*

The fans mobbing him had only rubbed salt in the wound. Soon Carter would need to announce his retirement to the world.

At the moment, he felt nothing. A numbness, like an impenetrable fog, cloaked him. He'd expected to feel angry, at the very least. Carter had heard stories of pitchers sobbing like little girls when they'd found out they had this kind of an injury. It was a player's worst nightmare—but it didn't feel like a nightmare. It simply felt unreal.

Carter wandered downtown Seattle, the crowds bigger now that it was the height of tourist season. People wearing suits walked amongst families wearing fanny packs, while the homeless dotted the corners, some taking up the entire side-walk. Carter lived in one of the high-rises near Pike Market that overlooked Elliott Bay, but he didn't want to go home right now.

He finally decided to get out of the city because right then it felt like it was choking him. He hadn't planned to drive south, but when he reached his old childhood home, where his dad still lived, he couldn't feel surprised.

Maybe he'd always needed to end up here.

The house was about fifty years old, well tended despite Mike Roberts's advancing age. He was what—seventy? Carter had lost track. He hadn't spoken to his dad in years, although apparently he'd gotten sober in the interim. Carter had only found out about his dad's sobriety because Mike had tried to contact him during his time in Alcoholics Anonymous. Apparently Carter had been one of Mike's twelve steps, but Carter hadn't been interested in being just another checkmark on his dad's list of attempted amends.

Carter knocked on the door, waited, then knocked again. When the door opened, Carter couldn't help the shock that rolled through him as he looked at his dad: older than Carter remembered, and now walking with a cane. But what was most striking of all was how much Carter looked like his dad, except younger and stronger.

"What do you want?" said Mike in a voice roughened by age and booze.

"Can I come in?"

Mike shrugged and opened the door further, allowing Carter inside.

The house hadn't changed much since Carter had been a kid: the same photos, now faded with age, hung on the wall. The carpet was the same worn brown, the walls yellow-beige. The only things that were new were the leather recliner and the huge flat-screen TV that was currently blaring *The Price Is Right*.

"Well, since you're here, you might as well sit down." Mike sat down and put his feet up.

Carter didn't sit; he wandered around the house instead. He still didn't know what he was looking for here. Maybe he'd come because he didn't want to be alone right now.

Lucy wouldn't have let you do this alone, he thought. But the last thing he wanted was for Lucy to see was how low he'd fallen. It was better this way. Lucy had texted him more than once, but he'd ignored the messages.

He shouldn't have slept with her last night, but he'd been weak. He hadn't had the willpower to send her away. But once she realized he was a nobody with a useless shoulder, she'd forget about him. She'd probably start dating Hayden like she'd always wanted.

That thought made him want to punch a hole in the wall. Instead, he went into his old bedroom, which was filled with his dusty baseball trophies from his Little League days. Multiple framed photos of Carter's various teams hung on the wall. He smiled when he found the medal he'd gotten for MVP when he'd been, what, eleven? That had been a great day. His dad had even tried to stay sober during Carter's celebration party, although he hadn't lasted more than three hours before he'd cracked a beer open.

Carter returned to the living room. A woman was screaming on the TV because she'd spun a dollar and would go on to compete in the showcase round.

"I'm retiring," said Carter. "From baseball."

Mike rocked slowly, his focus on the TV. "Really," was his reply.

"I tore my rotator cuff and it's not healed enough to let me play without seriously damaging my shoulder further." Carter laughed hollowly. "It's all over. Everything I worked for. Gone in an instant."

Mike just rocked, rocked, rocked.

"I heard about that on TV, about your shoulder." Mike glanced at Carter. "You coulda told me, you know."

"I didn't think you would've cared."

"Suit yourself." Mike shrugged.

Carter suddenly wished his dad would yell at him, like he had when Carter was a child. Had he come here so his dad could tell him he was a failure? How fucking twisted was that? Or maybe the child inside him had wanted the opposite. *It'll be okay, son. You're still worth something.*

Yeah, he was really fucked in the head if he'd expected something like that to happen.

"You know what? This was a stupid idea." Carter got up, shaking his head at both himself and his dad.

"I learned a lot of things about myself when I was getting sober," said Mike quietly. "And I know I wasn't a great dad to you."

Carter stopped, his hand on the door frame.

"But I pushed you to become a great player. That was me. Where would you be without me? You'd be working some minimum wage job, wasting your life away."

Carter felt that anger he'd been waiting to feel. And he reveled in it, because at least he had something to cling to right now. "Is that what you wanted to say to me? Well, thanks, Dad. You told me I was never good enough, a piece of shit, all of those things, but I guess it worked."

"You were always like this: whining about things. Now you're out, and what? You gonna sit and cry about it? Son, life is shit. Sooner you remember that, the easier it'll be for you."

Carter didn't stay to hear the rest of Mike's speech. There was no point, anyway.

He sat in his car for a while, remembering his childhood, and suddenly that anger he'd wanted so badly faded into the numbness from before. His dad was old, alone, and bitter, and Carter could see himself becoming like him if he weren't careful. It was a stark realization that settled in his stomach like a ball of lead.

He saw Lucy in his mind's eye. He groaned, resting his forehead against the steering wheel. He needed to see Lucy one last time, but what could he offer her? Nothing.

He was a washed-up ballplayer with a broken shoulder and with no future ahead of him.

~

A week passed without Carter responding to any of Lucy's messages. He hadn't called, and he hadn't texted. By the Monday a week after Carter had left for Seattle, Lucy didn't know what to do.

She'd told him that she loved him, and he'd said…nothing. He'd lied to her instead. She'd believed that he'd talk to her about their relationship later, but that later had yet to come. She told herself that maybe he was busy, that maybe his phone had fallen into Puget Sound, that maybe he'd been abducted by aliens. She almost wished he *had* been abducted by aliens: it would hurt less than the realization that he'd never cared about her at all.

There were only a few more days of filming. The excitement on set was almost contagious, but Lucy only felt dread. Once the crew packed up their things, there was no reason for Carter to return. She'd go back to LA and wonder why the man she loved had disappeared like a puff of smoke.

Her heart hurt. She'd already cried herself to sleep multiple nights. The only thing that kept her going was her work ethic and wanting no one around her to notice that she was breaking down inside.

Luckily for her, she was a good actress.

When she opened the door of her trailer after Tuesday's filming, she stopped in her tracks when she saw Hayden lounging on her tiny couch. Things had felt somewhat less strained between them, Hayden going so far as to talk to her during breaks like they were friends.

"Why are you in my trailer?" she said, frowning.

"I've been wanting to talk to you, but you keep sneaking off set the second we're done filming."

Lucy sat down across from Hayden, vaguely curious but too preoccupied to care much about what Hayden wanted. The more time she spent with Hayden, the more she realized how wrong he would've been for her. He was too conceited and thoughtless, no matter how handsome or how famous he was. She would've hated him within a month of dating him.

"I noticed that Carter isn't around. Did he go back to Seattle?" Hayden's question was casual.

"He did. Why do you ask?"

"Just curious. I'm still surprised you ended up messing around with him after what I'd told you about him and Rosie. You seem too smart for a guy like him."

Lucy rolled her eyes. "If you're trying to hit on me, don't."

Hayden put his hands up, smiling as innocently as he could. "Nothing like that. I swear. But he alluded to something I thought you should know. I already told you about our history, or his history with Rosie. Apparently he was more pissed off about that whole thing than I knew."

Ice started to spread inside Lucy. There was something in Hayden's eyes that made her want to throw him out of her trailer, but she was riveted to the spot.

"Apparently, Carter only started dating—well, fake-dating—you to get back at me. Hilarious, right? He's so desperate for revenge that he thought if he got into your pants, I'd lose it." Hayden's smile widened, and he chuckled.

Lucy's ears were ringing. "He told you this?"

"He did." Hayden got up and, standing over her, put his hand on her shoulder. "I'm sorry. I thought you should know before things go too far. You're a nice girl, Lucy, but people in this business are rarely nice. You have to watch out for yourself." He patted her shoulder before he left the trailer.

Lucy wondered why she couldn't breathe. Her heart pounded so fast she had to lie down to keep from falling over. Her mind whirled round and round, repeating Hayden's words inside her head. He'd known about her bargain with Carter, which meant that Carter must've told him. And based on Carter's complete silence after she'd told him she loved him, he had just been using her for revenge.

Hayden lied about Rosie, though, her brain reminded her. But had he? Or had Rosie lied to *him*?

Lucy's head hurt, and she felt sick. She wanted to cry, but the tears wouldn't come. She felt like she had the day that Glen had touched her in his office: dirty and discarded.

The only thing she could do was find Carter and demand answers—even if those answers destroyed her love for him.

CHAPTER EIGHTEEN

The day that filming wrapped, the cast and crew threw a party at Verity, the same restaurant where Lucy had agreed to her ridiculous bargain with Carter. It felt like years ago instead of weeks.

Hayden was all smiles at the party, even going so far as to throw his arm around Lucy's shoulders. Erin was already on her third martini, and even Jim was tipsy. Lucy had never seen Jim actually smile, so seeing him laughing now was slightly unsettling. She felt like she'd been thrown into Opposite World. Next Carter would show up and tell her he loved her and wanted her in his life.

Lucy snorted under her breath. Carter hadn't responded to her messages, and she knew now that he wouldn't. She wanted to confront him in person, but how could she when he was probably hiding out in Seattle? She could ask Anthony, but then she'd have to tell him why. That thought alone kept her from saying anything to her sister or to her sister's boyfriend.

Mostly she wanted to kick Carter in his kneecaps. Her

devastation at his desertion had morphed into rage at his betrayal. Each day he was silent was more confirmation that Hayden had told her the truth. He'd used her, and she'd fallen in love with him. She couldn't believe she'd been so stupid.

"You look way too sober," said Erin in a slurring voice. She sat down next to Lucy with a giggle. "Aren't you happy? We're done!"

"I have to get up early tomorrow," Lucy lied.

Erin tipped her martini glass back to catch the last few drops. "So, what's happening between you and Hayden?" She wiggled her eyebrows. "He can't stop hanging all over you."

"Nothing at this point. Sorry to burst your bubble."

Erin pouted. "I thought you were super into him? Wait, I know you were! Must've been because you were hanging out with Carter Roberts. Couldn't choose which hot guy you liked the most, I bet."

Lucy sighed. She decided she'd rather get a drink than listen to Erin babble about her sad love life. She considered leaving early and going to bed, but the thought of being alone in her room was worse than being here. It would only remind her of Carter. Tears sprang to her eyes without warning. She wiped them away hastily before anyone noticed.

"Hey, some of us are going down to the beach," said Hayden near her shoulder. "You wanna join?"

Considering it would be freezing, Lucy was about to say no when a voice answered for her. "She's coming with me."

Lucy's heart stopped. Turning, she drank in Carter's face, hating herself for wanting him still. Just to be contrary, she replied to Hayden, "I'd love to come. Let me get my coat."

Hayden glanced between them both, then put up his hands. "You guys have fun. I'm not getting in the middle."

"That's the first time he's done something smart," muttered Carter.

Lucy gripped the top of the nearest chair until her fingers ached. She couldn't help but notice that Carter seemed paler, and he had at least three days' growth of beard. He looked exhausted and almost defeated. Had he gotten bad news regarding his shoulder while in Seattle? Her heart broke at the mere thought. Was that why he'd been avoiding her?

"You can't just show up here out of the blue and expect me to follow you like some dog," said Lucy. Her eyes flashed. "Why have you been ignoring my messages?"

"I'd rather explain somewhere that isn't a bar full of people." Carter set down a few dollars for Lucy's drink and took her hand. "We're leaving."

His grip was firm enough that Lucy knew she wouldn't get free unless she caused a scene. Both curious what he had to say and annoyed she was giving in, she said nothing to him as they walked to the bed-and-breakfast.

Gwen stood at the front when they entered. Her eyes widened, and she shot a look of concern at Lucy. Lucy mouthed, *It's fine.*

When Carter shut the door to Lucy's room, Lucy gasped in surprise when Carter kissed her. Heat burst inside her veins, and if it weren't for the anger and hurt holding her up, she would've collapsed at his feet.

She pushed at his chest. "You don't get to kiss me without explaining," she gasped. She pushed harder at the muscled wall of his chest, but he wouldn't let her go. "Why are you even here? You ran out of here pretty quickly when I told you that I loved you." A flush climbed up Lucy's cheeks, and she couldn't help but look away in embarrassment. Her voice broke as she said, "You should've stayed in Seattle."

"I was going to, but I couldn't. You make me weak." He sounded resigned, and it scared Lucy. She didn't know how to respond to this Carter Roberts. What had happened to the confident and cocky Carter? She could tell that Carter to go to hell. She didn't know if this Carter would take such words very well.

"You sound like I've ruined your life." Lucy laughed sadly and finally moved out of his embrace. "But you have to tell me something first." She trembled as she remembered Hayden's words. *Carter used you for revenge against me.* "Why did you make that bargain with me, Carter?"

"You already know the answer to that."

She shook her head, anger building inside her chest. "I don't know anything anymore. Tell me the truth: why did you want to play my boyfriend? Was it just because you wanted to help pathetic little me, who couldn't get Hayden's attention without your help? Or did you really do it because you wanted to get revenge on Hayden?"

She watched Carter's face for his reaction, and when he paled, she knew. She *knew.* A cry of pain burst from her throat, and she slapped a hand over her mouth to keep from sobbing.

"Lucy, it wasn't like that—" Carter tried to touch her, but she wrenched herself from his grasp.

"Tell me what it was like, then. Tell me so I can understand."

Carter's expression was stark, and his chest rose and fell with quick breaths. "What did Hayden tell you?"

"He told me that you went out with me because you

wanted to fuck with him. That I was just a tool in your sick game of revenge." Lucy's bottom lip quivered, and the tears started spilling down her cheeks despite her best efforts to keep them at bay.

"Baby, it wasn't like that. I mean, it was, but things changed. Everything got complicated, and suddenly it wasn't about getting back at Hayden anymore. It was about you. About us."

"I'm supposed to believe that? When you lied to me after I told you that I loved you and then refused to talk to me? I can't believe anything you're saying now."

"I'm telling the fucking truth!" he burst out, his voice resounding through the small room. He gripped Lucy's fore-arms. "Look at me. Goddammit, Lucy, fucking *look at me*."

She looked at him, and her heart felt like it was shattering into a million pieces.

"I didn't know it ten days ago or weeks ago, but I love you," he said in a hoarse voice. "I'm in love with you, and I'm sorry things started out like they did. I never intended to hurt you."

Lucy felt the tears rolling down her cheeks, but she barely felt them now. "Everyone warned me about you. Men like you only think about using women for their own ends. I was so stupid to think that you were different."

His fingers dug into her wrists. "I am different. How can you think otherwise?"

"Do you know how you made me feel? Dirty. Used. Discarded. Just like Glen. You aren't any different from him."

"Fucking hell, Lucy." Carter let go of her wrists to take hold of her chin. "You're wrong. Glen never gave a damn about you. He never loved you and wanted to give you everything you ever wanted. He was a lowlife scumbag. Don't tell me we're the same person. Besides, you used me, too."

Lucy stared at Carter. "How? You consented to being used. I didn't. There's a difference." She slapped his hand away from her face.

"Lucy—fuck, don't turn away from me."

Lucy stared out the window, refusing to look at him. He didn't try to touch her again.

"I'm sorry," said Carter. "For the last time, I'm sorry. But you're choosing this, not me. Remember that when you lie down in your cold bed at night."

"This is over. Don't contact me again," she whispered.

"I won't. I can promise you that, at least."

Lucy flinched when Carter slammed the door as he left. She lasted ten seconds before her knees gave out, and she began to sob.

CHAPTER NINETEEN

"Luuuuuucy, dinner is ready!" called Thea from the kitchen. "I made vegan curry!"

Lucy bit back a smile at her sister's enthusiasm for all things vegan. Despite her trepidation, she had to admit that Thea could make damn tasty vegan dishes.

At the moment, though, Lucy wasn't hungry. She hadn't been hungry much in the last month since she'd broken things off with Carter. She'd inadvertently lost five pounds, which, considering how petite she was already, was enough weight that Thea had commented on it. Lucy had brushed aside her sister's concerns. The last thing she wanted to talk about was Carter and how he'd stomped all over her heart.

Lucy had decided to stay with Thea and Anthony in Seattle for a week. A week turned into two, and now she'd been here for a month. Thea had quietly offered to help Lucy break her lease in Los Angeles if she wanted to move back to Washington, but Lucy had demurred.

In all honesty, Lucy had no idea what she wanted to do. She was more lost than she'd ever been.

Lucy didn't say much as they ate, but Thea and Anthony kept up the conversation without her help. When Thea had invited her to come to stay with them, Lucy hadn't known what to expect being around her sister's boyfriend. He'd been nothing but polite to Lucy, going so far as to ask her more than once if she needed anything. In all respects, he treated her like a newly adopted sister.

"I told you that we were going to have to print a third run," said Thea in triumph. Her eyes sparkled as she looked over Lucy. "Anthony here thought nobody would buy the paperback version, but I told him that comic book lovers are obsessed with actual paper books still."

"Just because hardcore fans buy the paperbacks doesn't mean the general public will," said Anthony calmly. "All of our data said as much."

"Oh baby, I love when you talk data to me," purred Thea.

Lucy would usually find her sister's flirting with her boyfriend amusing. Lately, though, it grated on her. Mostly it reminded her of what she didn't have, and then she felt guilty for her envy. She should be happy for Thea—and she was. She also wished they weren't so blatantly in love with each other. It was like salt in her wounded heart.

"Lucy, I especially wanted you to come to dinner because Tony-kins and I have an announcement." Thea clapped her hands, almost bouncing out of her chair. Before Lucy could ask what it was, Thea blurted, "We're getting married!"

Lucy glanced at Thea's left hand and, seeing it still bare, frowned. "Did you not buy my sister a ring?" she accused Anthony.

Anthony rolled his eyes. "Thea refused to let me pick it out. She says I'd pick out the wrong one. We're going ring shopping tomorrow." In a kinder tone, he added, "You're welcome to come along with us."

"Oh, you should, Luce. I'd love to have your opinion," said Thea.

To Lucy's surprise, she felt her lower lip wobble. In a strained voice, she said, "Congratulations." She didn't even finish saying the word when she burst into noisy tears.

Nobody said a word. Humiliated and guilt-stricken, Lucy ran upstairs. How could she have ruined such a happy moment for her sister and soon-to-be brother-in-law? It wasn't about her. That made her cry harder, and she wished she'd gone to her tiny apartment in LA instead of coming here.

"Lucy, are you okay?" Thea came inside the guest room where Lucy was staying and immediately pulled Lucy into a hug. "What is it? Tell me."

"I'm sorry. I'm so happy for you. I really am." Lucy's statements with punctuated with watery sobs.

"I know you are, but I should've known. You've been a shell of yourself ever since you arrived. Something happened with Carter, didn't it?"

At the mention of Carter, Lucy cried harder. After going through almost half a box of tissues, Lucy finally calmed enough to tell Thea the entire sordid tale, including how Carter had used her for revenge.

"And I told him I loved him!" she wailed. "I'm so stupid. I could kick myself."

"Did Carter say it back to you?"

"Yes, but he didn't mean it. He couldn't have been serious."

Thea frowned. "You don't know that. And believe me,

guys like him don't throw those words around lightly. I would bet he meant it."

That statement only made Lucy feel worse. If Carter had loved her before, he obviously wouldn't love her now. Groaning, she fell onto the bed, her head pounding from her crying jag.

"I'm not going to tell you to forgive him, because what he did was shitty," said Thea. "Really, really shitty. But I also can't judge him, because I did something similarly terrible to Anthony. I almost lost him because of it. I would bet you Carter feels like there's nothing he can do to make up for what he did to you, but is one mistake worth tossing away everything you guys had?"

Lucy gazed up at her sister, dangerous hope blooming inside her. "Do you really think he loves me?"

"Based on everything you've told me?" Thea snorted. "He's got it bad. And if it helps, Anthony agrees with me. He's tried to talk to Carter, but he hasn't answered any of Anthony's messages."

"Doesn't that confirm he's over me?" Lucy crossed her arms. "I'm still pissed at him."

"Like I said, I'm not judging you. You have a right to be angry. But don't throw this away over one mistake. Love is the scariest thing ever, but wouldn't you rather know if there's still a chance for you two?"

Lucy almost preferred to believe that Carter didn't care about her now, because then she didn't have to face his possible rejection. The thought of him telling her she was nothing to him pierced straight through her heart.

Once again, she wondered if he'd gotten bad news regarding his injury, but most likely it would've been reported all over the news. So far, Lucy hadn't seen or read anything about Carter and his career. That meant he simply didn't want to see her again, based on his complete radio silence toward her.

Lucy sat up and hugged Thea. "I am happy for you. You deserve a guy like Anthony, even if he scares me."

"Anthony? Don't be scared of him." Thea chuckled. "He's a big softy. He cried watching *Homeward Bound* a few weeks ago. He was super mad when I made fun of him for it."

Lucy couldn't stop from smiling at that image. Then she sighed. "Can you tell me everything's going to be okay like you did when I was little?"

Thea petted Lucy's hair. "I can't tell you that, but I can tell you that I know you're strong and you'll figure this out. And if Carter wants to be with you and you want the same, then it'll happen."

Later that evening, Wendy called Lucy and left a voice-mail. *Hayden Masterson wants you to be his date at the premiere of his latest film. Call me and let me know if you want to do it, although I don't know why you'd say no. Obviously you made an impression on him. It'd be amazing exposure, Lucy. Okay, talk to you soon.*

Lucy didn't let herself spend too much time thinking about her answer. For the first time in over a month, she felt excited. This could be a huge break for her career: not only starring beside Hayden in *The Last Goodbye*, but attending his premiere with him, like they were equally in-demand actors. Hayden irritated her now, but who cared? It'd be for one night. Surely Lucy could manage one evening in Hayden's presence without throwing a glass in his face.

"Hey," said Lucy when Wendy picked up, "I'll do it. Get me a plane ticket and I'll be there by Friday."

WHEN CARTER HEARD his front door open and close when he wasn't expecting any visitors, he briefly wondered if a murderer had come to off him. Shrugging, he took another drink of his beer. It wasn't like he had anything going for him right now, anyway.

"Christ, it smells in here," said Anthony in disgust. He went to the nearest window and lifted the blinds, flooding Carter's apartment with overly cheery sunlight. The sound of traffic filled the room once Anthony had opened all of the windows, a fresh breeze only adding to Carter's irritation.

"How did you get into the building?" said Carter. He lived in a high-rise that had tight security—as it should, considering the amount of money that flowed through its doors.

"The guy who owns this building owes me money."

So much for security.

Anthony sat down on the leather armchair and put his feet up on the coffee table. "You look like hell, by the way."

"I'm aware." In the month since Carter had lost his entire career and Lucy, he hadn't exactly taken it well. He'd holed himself up in his apartment like some kind of pathetic hermit, drinking like a fish and disinclined to do anything productive. What was the point? He wasn't a baseball player anymore, and the woman he loved had thrown that love back into his face.

He was, in one word, a failure.

"I was going to let you mope as long as you wanted, but Thea was worried about you. So, here I am." Anthony raised an eyebrow. "How are you, by the way?"

Carter hadn't told his best friend about his forced retirement, nor had he told him the sordid details surrounding his relationship with Anthony's girlfriend's sister. Anthony pitying him would only make things worse.

"I'm alive," said Carter. "You want a drink?"

"It's three in the afternoon." It was the gentlest Anthony had ever spoken to Carter, and it only made him want to punch his friend in the face.

"Go fuck yourself. I'm not interested in hearing you sound like Dr. Phil or some shit," sneered Carter.

"Do you think I'd ever try to be your therapist? I don't like anyone that much." Anthony sighed. "I'm actually here because Lucy has been staying with us for the past month. I thought you'd like to know."

Carter felt his guts twist inside him, fear congealing around his heart. Forcing himself to be nonchalant, he shrugged. "What about her?"

"You know, I don't really give a shit about who you mess around with, but Lucy is Thea's sister. And considering I'm going to marry Thea, that makes Lucy *my* sister." Anthony leaned forward. "So, that gives me a right to beat you to a pulp for hurting her."

"You're engaged?" Carter couldn't help but be hurt that Anthony hadn't told him he was going to propose to Thea. But considering Carter had been avoiding everyone, including Anthony, he shouldn't be surprised.

"We are. You can congratulate me later. Lucy was a mess the entire time she was with us; even I could tell that, and I'm not exactly Mr. Feelings. Thea told me that Lucy is way too broken up about everything that happened not to be in love with you still. Now, Thea wouldn't tell me exactly why you two are acting like dumbasses because she didn't want me to get charged with murder. I'm going to assume the blame rests mostly on you."

"You don't fucking know anything." Carter stood up. "And what does it matter? I told her I loved her and she threw it in my face. Is that what you wanted to hear?"

"I'm not your enemy, despite what you might be thinking."

Carter stalked to one of the open windows. It was such a cheery, sunny day that it only soured his mood further. Why did the world continue on when he was disintegrating?

"I'm out, Tony," said Carter quietly, staring out at the horizon.

He'd gotten this place for its view of Elliott Bay, the snowy peaks of the Olympics often visible as well. Right then, it only reminded him of Lucy and Hazel Island.

Anthony swore quietly. He didn't need Carter to explain. "I'm sorry, man. I know you were hoping you could play again."

"I have a press conference this Saturday to tell the world I'm out completely." Carter felt anger well inside him: not only did he have to suffer the humiliation of his body betraying him like this, but he had to tell the public about it and act like he was going to be fine.

Anthony came up behind him and put a hand on his shoulder. "I told you I'm not going to play Dr. Phil with you, but I can't help but give you advice."

"Thea's made you soft." Carter scoffed.

"She's made me a better man, you're right. She saw something in me that I couldn't see for myself. I thank God every day that I got stuck in that damn cabin with her and she was willing to take a second chance on me." Anthony moved so he stood next to Carter, also gazing out onto Elliott Bay. "But you're not just baseball. You're more than your accomplishments or your failures. If that's why you're unwilling to get Lucy back, then you're going to end up regretting it for the rest of your life."

Carter wished Anthony would go away. He didn't want to hear profound statements. He wanted to wallow in his anger and disappointment until it swallowed him whole.

"I'm nothing without baseball and you know it," he said bitterly. "I can't do anything else."

"Who says you can't? Look, I get it. My company was everything to me. It defined me completely. When I had to let it go, I wasn't sure I could."

Carter shot his friend a wry look. "And you started another company right after. Doesn't count, dude."

"But I'm not the only one running it, and I actually take days off. It's different. If it imploded, I wouldn't implode with it."

Since when had Anthony turned into some wise old man? He really was Dr. Phil now. He'd be disgusted, if Anthony's advice weren't spot-on.

By the time Anthony said goodbye, evening was closing in.

Carter wondered if Anthony was right. Maybe he could live without playing baseball. The thought of finding fulfillment in something else filled him with trepidation. When your entire life had been focused on one thing and that one thing suddenly disappeared, it was if you had no foundation to stand on. It was all shifting sands that were terrifyingly unstable.

What gave Carter hope was the thought that Lucy missed him. He hadn't contacted her since she'd told him not to, and

Call me when you get a chance! Lucy's agent, Wendy, had texted her this morning. Apparently *The Last Goodbye* was already getting buzz, and there were multiple producers sniffing around Lucy. Lucy should be excited over the news, but she only felt numb and vaguely annoyed.

"Luuuuuuuuucy! Get your cute little butt down here!" said Thea.

Lucy knew her sister would force-feed her if she didn't come to dinner. Thea had always been something of a mother to Lucy, and now more than ever, Lucy saw how much her sister wanted to fix her problems for her; but she couldn't.

"I'm coming!" Lucy put on her fuzzy slippers and headed downstairs. Thea and Anthony lived in a three-bedroom condo on the west side of Seattle. Newly renovated, it had the biggest Jacuzzi tub Lucy had ever seen, along with huge windows that had a view of Mount Rainier. Lucy sometimes liked to sit in the living room before Thea and Anthony got up and simply stare at the mountains for a while.

"There you are! I was about to come throw you over my shoulder. Get a plate." Thea busied herself with serving everyone, like a housewife on steroids, as Anthony had called her last night. Thea had almost thrown a dinner roll at his head.

"It smells amazing." Lucy's stomach rumbled for the first time in ages.

"Do you want chicken or seitan? The seitan is way better, by the way," said Thea.

"It really isn't." Anthony grabbed his plate—with chicken, as he'd declined to share Thea's chosen diet—and kissed Thea on the cheek. "Thanks, babe."

"I'll take the seitan," said Lucy, mostly to make Thea happy.

he'd been too angry to grovel. Now he regretted that he hadn't begged her for her forgiveness weeks ago.

But if there was still a chance to get her back, he would. He had to. He realized in a flash that she was even more important to him than his career. She'd ransacked his very soul, breaking it open and revealing a side of himself he hadn't thought existed. It was humbling, that realization, and Carter wasn't exactly great friends with humility.

He knew what he had to do now; he just hoped that Lucy would give him a second chance.

CHAPTER TWENTY

Hayden tightened his arm around Lucy's waist. "At least act like you're enjoying yourself," he hissed in her ear.

He smiled his golden smile at the photographers, the constant flash of bulbs making Lucy a little dizzy. It could have also been that the multiple layers of shapewear she'd put on to fit into her dress were making her lightheaded. She felt like a stuffed sausage about to explode.

She'd decided to wear a backless red dress that showed off the light tan she'd gotten while on Hazel Island, her hair pulled back into a pretty chignon. The dress hadn't cost more than five hundred dollars, and Lucy had gotten it on sale two years ago. When Hayden had asked her who she was wearing, she'd lied and said it was the latest Versace, trying to bite back a giggle the entire time.

"I am enjoying myself," she hissed back. She pinched him hard on his lower back, and because they were in front of a huge crowd of photographers and fans, Hayden could only keep smiling.

This is for your career, Lucy kept telling herself. It had become her mantra for the evening to put up with Hayden's constant complaints and demands. When she'd met him at his mansion in Malibu, he'd barely said hello before he'd returned to his room to continue dressing. They'd ended up being two hours late to *his* premiere, although Hayden had blamed the traffic. *Since when is the 101 this bad this time of day?* he'd said over and over again.

Lucy had almost stuffed his tie into his mouth to shut him up. He'd also made snide remarks about her dress, her hair, and her person in general. Her dress didn't go with his tuxedo; her hair looked like she'd done it herself (she had done it herself). She didn't know why he was being this insufferable tonight, but she'd about had enough.

"You do that again and I'm tossing you out of here," Hayden said in a low breath as they entered the theater for the premiere.

Lucy rolled her eyes. If she could make it to the after-party at the hotel, she could get away from Hayden and hopefully introduce herself to other actors and industry people. As Wendy had reminded Lucy, it was all part of the game you played when you wanted a piece of the Hollywood pie.

As Lucy sat and watched the movie, she couldn't help but let her thoughts wander to Carter. She knew it was pointless, but he was like some kind of addiction. She couldn't purge him from her heart no matter how hard she tried to distract herself. Was he thinking about her? Or had he already moved on?

Of course he's moved on. If he really loved you, he would've tried to contact you by now.

She couldn't forget his betrayal, either. He'd used her like Glen had tried to use her, and although the initial rage had faded, the hurt remained because she'd trusted him. She'd given him her heart and he'd tossed it away without a second thought.

By the time she and Hayden arrived at the after-party almost three hours later, Lucy was desperate for a drink. Luckily she was able to slip away from Hayden easily, even though the party was absolutely packed. The room was a huge bar that had been decked out for the party, and Lucy had to remind herself to keep her mouth shut every time she recognized someone famous. After she got her drink, she was pretty sure she'd seen Leonardo DiCaprio walking toward the exit.

Lucy sat down at the bar, mostly because the party was so crowded she didn't have the energy to wade through the crowd of people. A man sat down next to her; when she saw that his suit was rumpled and his wallet was falling apart at the seams, she knew he wasn't anyone important. She wondered if he worked at the hotel and managed to sneak inside the party.

"You look familiar," the man said to her. "Do I know you from somewhere?"

"I doubt it. I'm not an A-lister."

"You were with Hayden Masterson tonight at the premiere." The man's eyes widened slightly in recognition. "You're Lucy Younger, aren't you? The up-and-comer."

Her lips lifted in a tight smile. "I guess that's me." She contemplated giving this guy an excuse that she needed to leave; she wasn't in the mood for him to try to hit on her.

"Can I buy you a drink? After you finish that one, of course," he said.

Lucy sighed. "Look, you seem like a nice guy, but I'm not on the market. Let's just put that out there, okay?"

The man didn't seem the least bit flustered. "Well, that's

good to know, because I'm married and not looking to hit on anyone." He flashed his left hand, where a gold band rested on his finger. "I'm Silas Martin, by the way."

Lucy's heart stopped. Silas Martin was one of the best directors in Hollywood right now. His latest film had been nominated for Best Picture at the Oscars two years ago. "Oh my God, I'm so sorry," she stuttered.

"No harm done." Silas pulled out a card from his jacket and handed it to her. "If you feel like talking, give me a call. I promise not to ask if you want me to buy you a drink, either."

Lucy let out a laugh right after Silas left. She couldn't believe her good luck. She couldn't help but think of how she'd put her foot in her mouth a second time in a month: Carter sure would've loved to hear about this second instance.

"Who was that?" said Hayden. He pointed to Silas's retreating figure.

"Silas Martin."

Hayden's eyes widened. "Seriously? I wanted to meet him." Hayden lurched forward into the crowd, clearly already inebriated.

After another hour, Lucy decided she needed some fresh air. When she got through the crowd into the hotel lobby, she let out a sigh of relief. It had been stiflingly hot in that room, even with the air conditioning blowing at full speed. She fanned herself and wandered until she reached a large room on the second floor where only a half dozen or so people were gathered.

She sat down and took off her stilettos, not caring if people were watching. Her feet ached and she was exhausted and starving. She was considering calling an Uber and getting some In-N-Out Burger when Hayden came stumbling toward her.

"There you are." He collapsed into the chair next to her, chuckling. "I can see your boobs down your dress when you bend over."

"Then don't look," she snapped.

"Then don't bend over." He shrugged, swirling his drink in his glass. "I bet Carter looked down your shirt all the time."

Lucy froze. Hayden hadn't mentioned Carter since that day he'd revealed that Carter was using her. Why bring him up now?

"He was disgusting about you," continued Hayden, his expression sneering. "Did you know he threatened me over you? I shoulda had him arrested." Hayden let out a belch.

Lucy couldn't breathe. "He threatened you? Why?"

"Because I knew you'd be an easy fuck and he got mad about it." Hayden's smile was lazy now. "I'd heard through the grapevine that you'd been fucking your way up the ladder. No judgment, you know. A girl has to do what she has to do. I was just surprised you decided to pick Carter over me."

"You didn't answer my question. What did Carter say to you?"

"What did he say? He said he'd fucking kill me, that's what he said." Hayden raised his arm, almost spilling his drink. "Then he fucking punched me. Piece of shit. If I ever see him again…"

Lucy didn't hear the rest of Hayden's diatribe. All she could think about was that Carter had defended her against the man he hated. If he'd wanted revenge against Hayden, wouldn't he have let Hayden screw with her instead? Her heart started pounding like mad.

"Did you hear me?" demanded Hayden, his voice rising. "Wanna go back to my place?"

Lucy realized right then that she didn't care about her career anymore, not if it meant she didn't have Carter in her life. Grabbing Hayden's drink from his hand, she dashed it into his face and said, "Go fuck yourself, Hayden. I'm done."

Hayden sputtered and swore, vowing revenge as Lucy ran downstairs. She pulled out her phone, almost dropping it in surprise when she saw the alert on her screen: *Orcas pitcher Carter Roberts out for good. What's next for the Seattle team?*

She wasted no time in clicking on the article, pulling up the video of the press conference. Carter sat in the middle, his expression more subdued than she'd ever seen it, and he announced that, due to his injury, he was retiring.

Lucy felt like water was rushing into her ears. He must've known he was out when he'd come back to Hazel Island, but he hadn't said a word. And she'd just yelled at him and treated him like he was the scum of the earth. She choked back a horrified sob.

After she'd gotten into the backseat of her Uber, she kept watching the video. The tears came with a vengeance when Carter leaned forward toward the microphone and said, "I have one last announcement." His gaze looked straight into the camera. "I want a certain someone to know that I'm sorry for everything, and that I love you. You're the best thing that's ever happened to me, little spitfire. I'm nothing without you."

She was hallucinating. Surely Carter hadn't said those things at his press conference? She didn't understand. Was he messing with her? Was it some elaborate joke?

But, no, she realized as she started crying harder. There was no reason for him to say such things unless he meant them. He'd gone before the world and declared his love for her without any hope that she'd reciprocate a second time. It amazed her; it broke her, in the best way possible.

Lucy was bawling by the time her driver reached her apartment. He asked her tentatively if she was all right. It took her a moment to say, "Take me to the airport. I just remembered I have a flight to catch."

Within three hours, she was on a plane going to Seattle.

CHAPTER TWENTY-ONE

After hours of his phone blowing up, Carter finally turned it off. He didn't need to explain himself to anyone. He didn't care that his manager was pissed at him or that his now former coach thought he was a complete idiot. *This was a press conference to talk about your career, not your fucking love life!* he'd bellowed in Carter's face.

Carter didn't give a shit. He'd never felt freer than when he'd uttered those words on live television. He hadn't even done it so that Lucy herself would hear them, although a part of him hoped she would. At the very least, he needed to find her and tell her how he felt, even if he took him saying the words until he was blue in the face. He had more than enough time now.

It was close to one a.m. when Carter heard a pounding on his front door. Frowning, he wondered if Anthony had come to berate him a second time. Carter threw open the door with angry words on his tongue that promptly died out when he saw it wasn't Anthony.

It was Lucy, wearing a red dress and soaked to the skin.

"Jesus Christ, get inside." Carter practically pushed her inside and grabbed a blanket from the back of the couch, wrapping her up in it.

"Carter," she said, her teeth chattering so badly that Carter could barely understand her. "Carter, I have to tell you something—"

"Not if you die of hypothermia first. Take off your dress." At Lucy's glare, he snorted. "Little spitfire, you know I love you naked, but you can't stay in that dress. Strip."

In the end, Lucy's hands were shaking too much, and she wore some ridiculous contraption that was like superglued to her body from getting wet. By the time Carter managed to get her naked, he'd felt like he'd run a marathon. He went and got some towels and more blankets until Lucy was so wrapped up only her face was exposed. Before she could protest, he pulled her into his lap and rubbed her arms until the shivering abated. She sighed, leaning her head against his shoulder.

"Now tell me why you came to my front door soaked like a drowned rat," said Carter.

Lucy scowled, which meant she was feeling more like herself. Taking off some of the blankets, she said, "I didn't think it would be raining. It never rains in July. We were under a drought warning!"

"As fascinating as discussing the summer weather in Washington is, I doubt that's why you came here. Or why you were wearing a dress like that."

"I was in LA for a movie premiere." She wouldn't look at him as she said the next words. "Hayden invited me as his date."

Carter barely stopped himself from dumping her from his

lap. "So is that how it is now? You came here to, what, ask for my blessing?"

"Don't be stupid. Of course not." Lucy stuck her pointy little chin out, which Carter found annoyingly endearing. "I would never date Hayden. He's an asshole." Her bravado faded as soon as it had appeared. "I saw the press conference." Her words were a whisper.

Carter closed his eyes. He'd wanted her to see that… hadn't he? Yet right that moment, he wished he'd kept his mouth shut. Especially if she was here to tell him there wasn't any hope for them.

"I wasn't thinking when I said that," he said, his voice like gravel. "But I meant every word."

Lucy's eyes shimmered with tears. "You still love me?"

"Is that what you came here to hear? Fucking hell, yes, I love you. It's eating me up inside. I can't forget you, and it's driving me insane." He gripped her arms as if he could keep her from disappearing again. "I love you, little spitfire. No matter what happens."

"Oh God." She burst into noisy tears. "I—love—you—too," she hiccupped. "I'm so sorry for what I said to you. Hayden told me that you defended me, and I knew he was the one who would've tried to use me. Not you."

Carter could only make out every other word Lucy said, but he didn't care. He'd heard "love" and "you" and those were the two most important words to him right now. He tangled his fingers in her wet hair.

"You love me," he repeated. "Say it again."

She smiled. "I love you. *I* love you. I *love* you. I love *you*." She giggled. "Isn't English fascinating? Different emphases on words can create completely different sentences—"

Carter shut her up with a kiss. Based on how she threw her arms around him, she wasn't offended in the least. He kissed her until he believed her, like he could taste the truth on her tongue.

"Wait," he said, looking at Lucy's dress on the floor, "did you come straight here from the premiere?"

"I got on the first flight out of LA." She beamed up at him.

"God, you must've made quite a scene at LAX in that dress. You probably made a few TSA agents' brains explode."

"Don't worry, I asked for a woman when they wanted to pat me down."

"Oh, that makes me feel better."

His attention was thoroughly diverted when Lucy shrugged out of the blankets, her skin now pink. She hadn't worn a bra with her dress, and Carter thanked whatever powers that be for that. He kissed her throat, loving the vibration of her moans against his tongue, before taking one of her breasts into his mouth. She shivered, especially when he bit down lightly on one hardened peak.

"You have the best tits I've ever seen," he groaned.

She laughed. "What a compliment." The laugh turned into a sigh when he pinched her other nipple and rolled it between his thumb and forefinger.

Carter wanted to savor her, but it'd been so long that he was already desperate to be inside her. When he found her soaking between her thighs, he knew she felt the same way. She arched into his touch like a flower seeking the sun.

He pushed the blankets off of her, tossing them into the pile of her clothes, and he palmed her ass with one hand and played with her sex with the other. She said his name, moving with his hand, and soon he felt her release slam into her. She tightened around his finger like she never wanted him to leave.

"I need all of you," she said. She undid his belt and freed his cock, and it pressed against her belly as he kissed her again.

"Take me, then." He sat back and watched her grasp his cock and notch it at her entrance. His eyes rolled back inside his head as she sheathed herself around him. It was pure ecstasy. It took everything in him not to lose it right then and there.

"I love you." She began to ride him, and Carter was reminded of the first time they'd slept together. Now, though, it wasn't pitch dark and he could see the flush in her cheeks, the bounce of her tits, the way she rolled her hips with every downstroke. She was a marvel. If he hadn't already known he loved her, he certainly knew it now.

"Little spitfire, you're everything I never knew I needed," he said with an honesty that could only come from intense physical pleasure.

He pushed her onto the couch and took over, thrusting inside her mindlessly, watching her face with every push of his cock inside her. She gasped and writhed. Carter had to hold her hips to keep her still. She cried out, a deeper flush climbing up her face.

He was already close, his release drawing tighter. When he came, he felt like he was pouring his entire self into this woman under him. A few seconds later, he felt that rhythmic tightening of her sex that meant her own release. It only prolonged his own until he was pretty sure he'd died when he finally rolled off of her, still inside her.

He belatedly realized he hadn't used a condom. He'd

never been that crazed with a woman before, and he said apologetically, "I didn't use protection. I wasn't thinking."

Lucy blinked. "Oh. Well, I'm on the Pill, so you're not going to get my eggo preggo." She cuddled close to him. "And I'm going to assume we're now monogamous, yes?"

He spanked her lightly, making her yelp. "That's a stupid question and you know it."

"I know." She caressed his face. "I only ever want to have sex with you from now on. How about that?"

"If another guy so much as looks at you, he's dead."

Her eyes widened. "Oooh, how possessive of you."

She wiggled, lifting her leg so it rested on his hip. The movement made him harden all over again, and he slowly began to thrust inside her. Her eyelids fluttered.

"I'm going to be the worst," he promised, picking up the pace. "I'm going to make you forget every man before me. I'm going to be inside of you constantly, until you beg me to leave you alone." He began to strum her clit; she arched her neck, which he licked. "I'm going to drive you insane like you've done to me and I'll never apologize for it."

"Hot sex with the guy I love all the time?" She squeaked when he pinched her clit. "Oh God, that sounds awful. I'm calling the police."

That earned her a nice slap on the ass for her cheek. "You're a fucking brat."

"You've told me that already like five thousand times." Her voice trailed off as she shuddered and came. Carter could only smirk as he made her come so many times she really was begging him to leave her alone—at least for a few minutes.

Later that night—more accurately, very early the next morning—they lay in Carter's bed together. Lucy was fast asleep, her fingers entwined with his. Carter listened to the patter of the rain against his window. He kissed Lucy's forehead, thankful for that crazy night at the bar in Hazel Island two months ago, when he'd made that deal with Lucy, never knowing it would change the course of his life forever.

The day Lucy had woken up feeling tired and sick to her stomach, she'd attributed it to nerves. But her symptoms had continued even after she'd gotten the part in a Silas Martin project, and she'd been so on edge that she'd started crying last night when she'd burned the lasagna. Carter had looked at her like she'd sprouted two heads.

It had been three months since that night when Lucy had shown up at Carter's door, soaked to the skin and bursting with love for him. At the moment, she lived primarily in Seattle with Carter while traveling to LA for auditions when necessary. She'd given up her apartment in LA without hesitation, because who wanted to live in a glorified dump when a girl could live in her boyfriend's gorgeous and stupidly expensive place in Seattle?

Carter had recently decided to start coaching. Lucy had suggested it, because Carter wasn't the least bit interested in a regular job. He didn't need a job for money (lucky him), but Lucy could see how bored and restless he was doing nothing. Finally annoyed with him deciding to reorganize her underwear drawer simply for something to do, she'd told him to get a job or she'd throw him out on his ear.

"You can't throw me out of my apartment," he'd drawled in amusement. "I own it."

"I'm pretty sure there's a law that says I can throw out my boyfriend for being a pain in the ass."

"The feeling is entirely mutual, babe."

She'd gotten her revenge for that statement, although by the end, Lucy hadn't been sure who'd enjoyed themselves more.

Lucy's symptoms weren't going away, though. She finally gave into Carter's badgering and went to the doctor. She was pretty sure she had some virus, and she'd spend some ungodly amount for a doctor to tell her to get some rest and drink plenty of fluids.

So when Dr. Giamatti came into the freezing cold exam room and said, "You're pregnant," Lucy burst into laughter.

"Are you sure?" Lucy said hurriedly. "Because I'm on the Pill, and I haven't missed a dose. And I know all about not taking it with an antibiotic."

Dr. Giamatti, a woman about twenty years Lucy's senior, shrugged. "Birth control isn't one hundred percent effective. Did you ever take your dose at a different time of day? That can affect it, too."

Lucy thought back, remembering the day she'd forgotten and hadn't taken her dose until five hours after her usual time. She groaned. "It was *one time!*"

"It only takes one time." Dr. Giamatti patted Lucy's knee. "Believe me, you aren't the first 'it was only one time' I've seen in here, and you won't be the last."

Lucy felt dazed as she returned home. She had no idea

how Carter would react. They'd barely discussed marriage, let alone kids. Would he be upset? Her stomach turned and she had to run to the bathroom to throw up. Well, at least she knew it wasn't the flu, she thought morosely.

When Carter came home four hours later, he kissed her and went up to shower. Lucy felt her anxiety growing with every passing minute she waited to tell him. She was going to wait for him to finish, but his shower seemed to go on and on. And on. Was he shaving his legs in there? Irritated, Lucy marched into the bathroom and yanked the shower curtain aside.

"Damn, Luce!" Carter dropped the bar of soap. "You scared the shit out of me." His expression turned lascivious. "You should join me and make up for it."

Lucy didn't hear him. She felt the words bubble up and fall free, until suddenly she was almost yelling, "I'm pregnant, you dumbass!"

The only sound was the water running. Lucy also felt her heartbeat in her ears, and when Carter didn't say anything, she started crying.

"I knew you'd react like this! Oh my God!" She ran from the bathroom to their bedroom, locking the door behind her.

It only took ten seconds for Carter to start pounding on the door. "Dammit, why the fuck did you lock the door? Dorothy Lucille Younger, open the door!"

Lucy regretted having ever told Carter her full name, only because it reminded her of her parents scolding her. "Go away!" she yelled.

When Carter started kicking at the door, Lucy let him in, a scowl on her face.

"What the hell was that about?" he demanded. He had a

towel wrapped around his waist, but he was still dripping wet, a puddle forming on the hardwood floor. "Were you serious?"

"Of course I was serious!" Lucy sat down on the edge of the bed, covering her face with her hands. She didn't want him to see her crying. "I found out today," she mumbled.

She heard Carter approach; he peeled her hands from her face. Drops of water splashed onto Lucy's jeans. When she looked up into his face, the shock had been replaced with something that could only be called wonder.

"You're serious," he said again. He glanced at her still-flat stomach. "You took a test?"

"Yes."

"You aren't just messing with me?"

She rolled her eyes. "It isn't April first, so, no."

To her surprise, he kneeled in front of her, bracketing her with his forearms. At this height, their faces were level. Lucy could make out every passing emotion in Carter's face.

"You're pregnant." His hands shook a little as he cupped her face.

Tears started rolling down Lucy's cheeks again. "I didn't know if you'd be happy about it or not."

"How could you ever think that?" He brushed the stray tears away. "I mean, I'm shocked, but if you think I'm not also so happy I could explode, you're wrong."

Lucy's lower lip wobbled. "I love you. I'm sorry."

"You don't have to apologize for anything." He kissed her, the taste of him calming her fears. She wondered in a stray thought if pregnancy made her extra emotional. Well, that meant Carter was in for a hell of a ride if she was going to cry at the drop of a hat now.

Lucy took his hand and put it over her belly. "I'm about two months."

"I thought you were on birth control?"

"I was. I am. But you got me pregnant anyway."

He looked so damn pleased with himself that Lucy pinched his arm.

"Damn. I don't think I've ever felt prouder," he said.

"You're such a man." Sighing, she ran her fingers through his wet hair. "How are we going to manage this? I'll probably be showing by the time we start filming. What if I get fired for being pregnant? Oh God!"

"Baby, take a deep breath. Another one. One, it'll be fine. Second, I'm pretty sure it's illegal to fire a woman for being pregnant. I mean, it isn't 1960 anymore."

Lucy giggled. "You're so sexy when you talk feminism."

As she imagined everything they'd have to do with a baby coming, she groaned and collapsed onto the bed. This gave Carter the opportunity to climb on top of her. He'd also lost his towel in the interim. Lucy couldn't help but squeeze his cock, which was already at attention.

"You're all wet," she complained.

"And I'm about to make you all wet, too." He yanked her jeans down to her ankles with a practiced movement. When he delved inside her panties, it didn't take long for his declaration to become true.

"I love you," she gasped, arching against his hand. "Our kid is going to be terrifying, you know."

He leaned down to kiss her, but not before rumbling, "I wouldn't have it any other way."

ABOUT THE AUTHOR

A coffee addict and cat lover, Iris Morland writes sexy and funny contemporary romances. If she's not reading or writing, she enjoys binging on Netflix shows and cooking something delicious.